LIFE IN ITS OWN FRAME OF REFERENCE

BY

Brenda Drexler

Published by Brenda Drexler

Aunt Dottie's Ghost

I'm sitting in the back seat of Mom's car trying to not hear any of the lame stuff they talk about. They are probably average lame parents, just like it's always been Mom's car and Dad's truck. My parents are funny like that; everything else is ours. I'm not really listening to them talk until Mom and Dad both laugh a little. It's really when Mom says, "Shush," to Dad, that my ears wake up. I know what that means. They don't want me to know something, and I can't stand that.

I'm trying to untangle a group of metal links that will prove how smart I am, based on how long it takes me to break them loose, without actually breaking them. Anyway, I'm just not looking too smart so far.

"What?" I ask. No one says anything. "What are you shushing Dad about, Mom?"

"Oh, it's nothing, Drew. Really. "

"But you guys were laughing, so it must be funny. I want to hear, too."

"Okay," says Mom. "But you must not mention it. We don't want to hurt anyone's feelings. Okay?"

"Sure. I'm not telling anyone anything. What is it?"

"Well, it's no big deal. It's just that every year for the last few years your Aunt Dottie has said that her friend, George, is going to come to Thanksgiving dinner, but he never shows. Occasionally, she seems to be talking to someone when no one is there. But, she doesn't seem upset that this George fella never shows up for dinner. I guess we shouldn't laugh at poor Aunt Dottie's expense; I suppose she has a little old-timers and doesn't know what she's saying sometimes."

Honestly, adults laugh at some lame stuff. It's taking all my might to be polite and keep listening. When Mom finishes about Aunt Dottie, I ask in disbelief, "So, that's what you and Dad were laughing about? Sorry, I don't get it."

"Then don't butt into our conversations, young man. And make sure you don't say anything to upset your aunt."

No problem. Geez. What the heck do they see funny in all that? So George somebody never makes an appearance. More food for me. Thinking about food makes my stomach growl. I will eat just about anything put in front of me on Thanksgiving so that I can eat all the desserts later. Boy I love desserts.

"Are we close yet? I'm starving."

***

We are just turning down my Aunt's long gravel driveway when I remember something I heard last Thanksgiving. "Hey Mom," I say to get her attention. "Wasn't Aunt Dottie in the circus a long time ago? What was she, a lion tamer?" I snicker because I think that's hilarious.

Mom turns her eyes on me. "Now don't go and bring that up today. Aunt Dottie will want to tell circus stories, and they are all just awful. Dirty animals, freak shows."

"That sounds really cool. But, what kind of work did she do?"

I can see Mom was getting tired of my questions. I gave her the big innocent eyes that usually win her over.

"Okay, okay. She was a fortune-teller. She had a crystal ball and the whole deal. Didn't last too long, though. She got homesick. Nuf said."

I have a feeling there is more to it than Mom is letting on, but maybe I can find out later.

***

Aunt Dottie bends over and gives me a bear hug. "Mmph." She pushes the air out of me; happens every time. There's Cousin Lillie, who is about the same age as Mom, and her whole family. I sure am glad they're already here because Tommy and I will be able to mess around out back before dinner. Gotta get through all the bear hugs first, though. Thank goodness Uncles don't do that; they smack me on the back or rub my head, even at 15, around here I'm still treated like I'm seven. Will probably have to sit at the kid's table again. Gotta wait for someone to die to move up.

After Tommy and I high-five each other and insult each other, "You're uglier than a turkey neck," and "You walk like one," we hover over the dessert table, which is filling up more and more each time the front door lets more family in. We used to be able to sample small amounts of icing and such without getting into trouble, but getting older has its drawbacks.

"You boys make yourselves useful and go find us some more chairs," orders Aunt Dottie.

"Man," complains Tommy, "we have to be useful nowadays. Turning fifteen should be more fun. We're almost grown men and still get treated like babies around here."

We make our way back to the kitchen, each of us dragging one chair behind. Suddenly, I see fun about to happen. He must have come in while we looked for chairs. He just set down a huge pot of something and is high-fiving the menfolk and hugging the women. The largest man I've ever seen in my life.

"Hey Uncle Moose, bet you can't catch me." I run out the door with Tommy right behind me.

Uncle Moose is after us before the screen door can slam. He always catches us, and we love it. His hulking body carries the both of us, one under each arm, kicking and laughing, to the barn, where he throws us right into a pile of hay. We try to get up, he picks us up again. The last time he actually gives us a choice.

"Okay, Drew, the hay or the chicken coop?"

"Hay," I plead, "the hay."

"Throw him in the chicken pooper," yells Tommy.

He throws me up into the air, and I land right beside Tommy, who also chooses the hay over the stinky chicken-poop coop. We're both laughing so hard we struggle to get up again.

"I guess that's enough punishment for now, boys. You two are getting almost too big for me. Now, if your Aunt Jo will let me, we can throw some ball later." He leaves the barn, chuckling.

"Wow! He is the greatest uncle," Tommy says as he picks hay out of his hair.

"Yeah. He is. He makes family get-togethers bearable."

We chase a few chickens around to avoid the house and possible work until Mom calls out the door, "Come to dinner, boys." We hit the dirt running.

One look at me, a scary look, and Mom says, "You touch nothing, young man, and I mean nothing. As soon as we say grace, you head to the hall bathroom and clean yourself up. Every stitch of clothing off and every piece of hay, or whatever, gone. Understand? And don't leave a path of filth as you go."

Oh, yes, I understand. Mom doesn't like the outside coming inside. Cousin Lillie isn't as picky, so Tommy gets to sit at the table before me and eat before me. Bad enough we have to sit with babies at the kid's table; even they get to eat before me.

I head to the bathroom, picking up hay along the way that falls off my shoes. When I'm a parent, what an awful thought, but if I ever am, I'll let my kids have fun. There's nothing wrong with a little hay. I stopped and looked around, thought I heard something... like a shuffling noise. I glance at the dark space under the steps...creepy, never noticed that before. "Oh well, probably hearing the echo of my own shoes on the rickety hardwood floor."

I have to admit, I'm pretty funny looking when I see myself in the mirror. I look more like a scarecrow than myself. I reach up and pull a piece of straw out of my ear. Okay, maybe Mom is right about me needing a little cleaning up. I hold my arms in the air like a real scarecrow. I get most of the hay and dirt off my clothes and out of my hair and make for the kitchen. Then I stop in my tracks.

"Wow. Good cleanup job," a voice from nowhere comments.

I nearly jump out of my skin as I close the bathroom door behind me, ready to fill my empty stomach, not to get nearly scared to death. I can't see anyone. "Who is that? Where are you?"

"Um," comes from the dark corner under the back stairs. I squint harder to help me see. Looks like there might be someone sitting back there.

"Someone there?" I ask, cautiously going closer. "Who are you?"

"Um," comes again from the dark corner. "Can you hear me? I didn't think you could. Most people can't." He sort of talks like he's scared of me, so I take one more step forward.

"Of course I can hear you. Why wouldn't I?"

My jaw drops, and I freeze in place. I now can see him, I think.

"Are … you … a …." I can't seem to finish, can't quite make myself say the words. So I stand there gulping, rocking back and forth, looking down the empty hallway for my escape, not sure of my next move.

"Yeah, I am. Well, if you meant to ask if I'm a ghost, that is. I'm mighty glad to make your acquaintance. My name is George. What's yours?" He's talking to me like nothing is unusual, like I meet ghosts every dang day.

"Um," is all I can say. I take one more step forward and peer deeper into the dark corner, which isn't nearly as dark, now that I've been staring there for so long.

"You're George? Aunt Dottie's George, who never," I have to chuckle just a little at this, "makes an appearance?"

"I reckon that's me. So you've heard of me. I have to say I feel honored to be so well known. All this time I've been hiding from the family; I don't want to freak anyone out. But, you're rather special, you know. Most people can't see ghosts, even if the ghosts want them to. You and Dottie have a gift, that's for sure. So, what's your name? By your age, you've got to be Tommy or Drew."

"Seriously," still in disbelief, "you're really a ghost?"

"Well, what the heck do you see? I'm guessing Tommy. Come on over and have a seat if you want. Plenty of room."

"I'm Drew."

He sure seems happy to talk to a live person. More so than I to a dead one.

"So you are only sort of invisible," I say as I move closer, yet. "You're sort of a clear balloon-man, aren't you? Yuck!" I yell. "Is that cranberry sauce floating around in your belly, and stuffing? Wait a minute. This means that you got to go to the table before me, too. That's not even right."

George chuckled. "Aw, don't be a spoil-sport. Here, have one of my biscuits," as he hurls one in my direction.

I catch it. "Mm, love aunt Dottie's buttery biscuits. Thanks. Good throw. I never would have thought that ghosts could eat, actually. But I have to say, George, it's sot of gross seeing your food just sitting there, for the whole world to see. You ever consider putting on a real shirt, or something?"

"Sorry, don't mean to offend anybody. I do it for your aunt. She's so nice, and we don't get in each other's way. She hasn't tried to get rid of me and isn't scared. She wants me to eat, so I eat a little. Make's her feel needed. Want some apple pie?" He stretches out his see-through arm toward me, holding a plate with a huge piece of pie covered in whipped crème.

I eat that pie with my fingers while George tells me about meeting Aunt Dottie. She knew he was in the house before he knew she knew. "She about scared me out of my skin," he stops to laugh at that. "One day she just jumped up in my face and yelled, BOO! She about scared me to death. Oh, wait. She couldn't do that, either, could she? Anyway, she made me jump a foot off the ground, for sure."

"That's funny." I lean against the wall, licking the apple pie off my fingers. "What are you doing here, George? Do you have some unfinished business to take care of, like the ghosts in movies?"

"Naw. Not me. I just like this place. I've lived here for, oh, say, about a bunch of years, or so. I raised chicks just like your Aunt Dottie does. You see, I lived a good life so I got the option to hang out here for about as long as I want to stay on this sweet earth. And that's what I'm doing. Yep, I really love this place."

"Wow. That's so awesome. How did you die? I'm assuming you did ... don't want to be too forward or rude about it. And, if you don't mind."

"You know what, Drew, this is Thanksgiving. And I'm so darned thankful to have met you that all I want to think about are my blessings. I never imagined that I would have good people in my... uh, life, after my life. That's sort of a weird thought, isn't it?"

We both laugh.

"Yeah, it is pretty weird. But so is talking to a genuine ghost. But I'm glad I met you, too. Do you think I'll meet more ghosts since I have this special gift that you mentioned?"

"Hard to say. I don't know much about it beyond my experience. I mean, you and your aunt are the only living people I know."

"If I do see other ghosts, will they always be able to see me, and will they be nice like you?"

"I expect so. Why not?"

"So, if I can come visit Aunt Dottie some other time, will you be here?"

"Sure I will. I've got a lot of time left here, if I want. And now I really want. Do you play chess, Drew?"

"Not yet. But I'll start learning tonight. Hey, man, I hate to go, but I'd better get to the kitchen or Mom will be looking for me. This is my best Thanksgiving ever, thanks to you, George. I never in my life thought I would actually talk to a real ghost."

He smiles, "And I never thought that I would be a ghost." We both laugh.

***

"Where did you get that biscuit?" Mom asks as soon as I walk into the room. "And what took you so long?"

"I was really dirty, just like you said. I'm starving!"

"What the heck?" Tommy looks at me like he's mad. "I've been sitting here with babies all this time, eating all alone, with no one to talk to, watching Uncle Moose's kid blow peas out her nose. Gross."

"Wait," I say. I walk over to Aunt Dottie and lean over to whisper in her ear. She turns with a huge smile on her face and gives me another bear hug. This time, I don't mind at all.

"Happy Thanksgiving, Drew," Aunt Dottie says. "You need to talk to your Mom about spending some of your Christmas holiday with me."

"Sure thing. Can hardly wait!"

I sit at the kid's table across from Tommy. "Let the food frenzy begin. Hey, giggles, show me how you blow peas out your nose."

"Uhg,"Tommy moans, then flips mashed potatoes right between my eyes.

***

I look out the rear window as the car pulls away from Aunt Dottie's place. There on the porch stands Aunt Dottie waving and throwing kisses. George stood next to her, waving and smiling. I can hardly wait for Christmas break.

Who Killed the Sod?

Most everyone, except for the judge, was already sweating and irritable, as the trial had started forty minutes late while maintenance tried to repair the air conditioner. The stifling heat accentuated the always-musty smell of the old courthouse. Some wiped away sweat while others sneezed and sniffled due to mold and dust.

"All rise. The Honorable Judge Silliman presiding." The small courtroom was nearly full. Three plaintiffs, three attorneys, the bailiff and a slew of other people with various reasons for attending this juryless proceeding filled the benches.

The young couple, John and Marci Baker, who sat as the first plaintiffs who got this whole thing rolling, huddled together with their attorney, Mr. Shifly, who looked miserable in his pin-striped suit. Must have had a more important case after this, because most people dress casual to trashy for small claims court. Although the cool air had started to roll into the courtroom, he continued to dab his forehead and the back of his neck. Marci had found a ponytail holder in her purse and had knotted her long black hair at the nape of her neck, and occasionally blew air down the front of her tank top. Her husband, John, pulled at the neck of his black t-shirt and fanned himself with his sod receipt, part of the evidence.

The Bakers are suing Daryl Cook, the man who laid their sod. He sat at the other table with his attorney, Mr. Cross. While Cross checked his cell phone, Cook glared at the Bakers and chewed, menacingly, at his upper lip.

The third plaintiff, Mr. Frye, sat with his attorney, Mr. Slight, at an added third table farther to the left, or right, depending on how you looked at it. Mr. Frye squirmed in his seat and mumbled under his breath while his attorney gave him the evil eye, and finally had to say, "Shut up, for God's sake. You're going to get on the bad side of the judge right off. He can't stand people making racket in his court."

"I'm Judge Silliman and this is my court," Judge Silliman announced. He stood, leaning on the huge mahogany podium "And I'd like to know who is here today. Keep it brief, but as you go around the room, state your name and your purpose for being here. If you have no real purpose, you can leave now."

The first to speak was a woman in her sixties. She looked very prim in her light linen jacket, tan shirt, and black slacks. She opened her mouth and closed it without making any noise. She tried again, "I'm Mrs. Brown, Your Honor. A witness and a neighbor of the Bakers." She glanced in their direction, briefly, and smiled her thin-lipped smile.

"What the hell is she doing here," whispered John to his wife. She shook her head to remind him to be quiet.

"What's your purpose here, Mrs. Brown?" The judge peered at her over the top of his glasses.

"Um. I'm testifying," she glanced in the direction of the sod layer, " for Mr. Cook, Your Honor." She smiled and crossed her hands on her lap. She gave the Bakers another quick glance, then focused on the judge.

"Next," said the judge, as he looked at the tiny man in a plaid shirt and denim jeans that ended in a pair of cowboy boots.

He coughed and sniffed before he spoke. "I'm Clyde Strong, sir, um, Your Honor. I bought sod from Fred, over there, in the past. I guess I'm a witness on behalf of Fred Frye." He cleared his throat.

The next person in the row across from Clyde spoke up as the judge looked at her and raised his eyebrows. "Your Honor, my name is Rachel Roberts. I'm an appointed court observer."

He made an odd, wrinkly-lipped face, and responded, "Hmph. In case anyone is wondering what a court observer is, they are here to observe whether we are doing our jobs properly, by using a checkoff list. Is that correct, Ms. Roberts?"

"Sort of, Your Honor. We do have an intense training about..."

"Thank you. Next"

The next person watched the judge smirk at Rachel Roberts, giving the impression that he didn't like court observers very much.

"Your honor, my name is Diana Marshall, and I, too, am a court observer." She felt a little nauseous and was glad he moved on, without comment, to intimidate the rest of those present in his court.

~.~

"Do you swear to tell the truth, the whole truth, and nothing but the truth?"

"I do." John Baker looked confident as he settled into the witness chair and smiled at his lovely wife, who smiled back.

"Please state your purpose here, Mr. Baker," his attorney requested.

"Yes." John cleared his throat. "Well, my wife, Marci, and I recently moved into our new home. Relocated from Pulaski County after we won a small lottery. Well, at least large enough to get us a new house." He chuckled. "Everything seemed to be going so well, not like the nightmare I'd heard other people talk about who had their homes built. Then we contracted with Daryl, or Mr. Cook, to lay our sod on all our property....half an acre. We were being very conscientious with everything as this was our first home, you know?

So, we watered the grass, or sod, every day. Next thing we know, it turns brown and crunchy. Just gone like a light. I mean, quickly."

"What did you do then?" asked Shifly.

"Of course, I called Mr. Cook. Seemed like the most reasonable thing to do. Don't ya think? Well, he came to look at the grass and shook his head and said that there was nothing he could do. Said that the heat or dry-spell or whatever burned it up was an act of God. Blamed God for my dead grass. My poor wife was beside herself, so I told him he was responsible for putting down healthy grass. My neighbors' grass didn't look like that. He told me to water it night and day, and it might come back green. So that's why we're here. It's toast."

Marci Baker had her arms across her chest and nodded her head in agreement with everything her husband attested to.

Mr. Cook bit his upper lip some more and sneered at the young man as he left the stand.

Mr. Frye looked disgusted over the whole matter.

Mr. Cook got to tell his side of the story, stating, "I tell you, that the grass looked good when I put it down in the Baker's yard. All I can figure is that they either didn't take care of it, or Mr. Frye sold me diseased sod." He leaned back in his seat and crossed his arms over his chest as if that was the end of the story.

"So, to sum this up," said the judge, "you, Mr. Baker, are suing Mr. Cook for putting down, what you think was, unhealthy sod that is now brown. And you, Mr. Cook, deny responsibility for the dead grass, but are suing Mr. Frye for selling you diseased sod, that you may or may not have put down in the Baker's yard. Does that sum it up for now?"

"Yes, your Honor," both Cook and Baker responded.

Mr. Frye stated under oath that he never sold anyone bad sod, and that he'd been in business for fifteen years without a complaint. He then said, "Cook can darn well find his sod somewhere else, because I wouldn't sell him a blade of grass after being called a cheat by him. Seems to me he's the cheat here."

"Who you calling a cheat, you old coot of a sod farmer?" Cook yelled.

"They're both cheats, if you ask me," chimed in John Baker.

"Yeah, they're both cheats," Marci shouted as she jumped out of her seat and grabbed her husband's arm.

The courtroom was in an uproar by then, as the sod layer and the sod grower threw out multiple accusations, while attorneys tried to get their clients under control and in their seats. The bailiff looked to the judge for direction. And the court observers were taking their responsibilities seriously and were making notes. No one heard the gavel pounding at first. But, as fate would have it, the very moment everyone quieted down, Diana Marshall, who was taking it all in with disbelief, said loud enough for all to hear, "They're all guilty!" She looked utterly shocked that the words came out of her mouth. She was thinking them, but didn't intend to actually say them. But there they were, echoing around the old court room, seeming to bounce off of one wall then the next.

The court was silent as every head turned in her direction. The judge gave her a stern look. But, before he could say anything, she took in a deep breath through her nose, opened her mouth like there might be something she needed to say, changed her mind, and rushed out of the court, leaving her friend, Rachel, to stare at the door as it shut behind her.

Judge Silliman slammed his gavel and shouted, "We'll take a fifteen-minute break. And I expect no more outbursts from anyone. I'm beginning to think that court observer was right."

After a brief break, Clyde Strong swore that Mr. Frye had always been honest in their business dealings. "I only work with honest men, Your Honor." Then he gave up the stand for Mrs. Brown.

"I live next door to the Bakers and saw when their sod went down. It looked just lovely, until they took off for vacation." She sniffed and crossed her arms as if that explained everything.

"What happened then?" asked Cook's attorney.

"Well, it didn't get watered. I told them it was going to be very hot. Even offered to water for them, but they turned me down. I was just trying to be helpful." She flashed a wicked smile and a raised eyebrow toward the Bakers. "They were always acting too good to be friendly, so I sure didn't bother to throw any water on their grass, even though I knew it would dry up. Too bad for them."

"Thank you, Mrs. Brown."

"Mrs. Brown," said the Baker's attorney, "I have just a few questions for you." He smiled a toothy smile. She smiled back and blinked her eyes. "So, since the Bakers didn't appreciate all your attempts at friendship and being a helpful neighbor, you decided it would be best to ignore their yard. Is that right?"

"Absolutely. I don't know if they thought they were better than me, or what."

"So, at that point you didn't care if their grass lived or died, did you?"

"Heck no. They deserved what they got. That's what I think."

"Mrs. Brown, can you remember prior neighbors who lived across the street from you? They moved away after only six months. A young couple, the Knights."

Mrs. Brown wrinkled her brow and pursed her lips. "What… what do you mean? That has nothing to do with this. They're gone already."

"Actually, Rhonda Knight is on her way here, at this very moment, to testify. Your Honor, if I may, I wish to add two witnesses on behalf of the Bakers." He turned back to Mrs. Brown and smiled again. She didn't. "You remember the Knights had an ongoing problem with their house? It became infested with roaches. That was shortly after a falling out with you, wasn't it?"

Mrs. Brown appeared ready to explode. She breathed heavily through her nose and glared at her questioner. Her brow perspired. Her eyes flitted around the room. Her face grew red. The courtroom was still. All attention was on the nervous Mrs. Brown. "I don't have to listen to this malarkey," she squeaked.

"I'm afraid you do." She glanced at the judge who had his chin resting on his knuckles, intent on the conversation.

"Mrs. Brown, you might be interested to know that the second witness, who should arrive any minute now, is a current neighbor. She has agreed to testify, under oath, that she did, indeed, see you water the Baker's lawn once while they were gone. Do you remember that?"

"There was no reason for them to be mean to me. I just wanted to be a friendly neighbor. They deserved what they got."

"Are you saying that they deserved for their sod to die, and that you decided to help it along? Is that what you're saying? What did you spray on the sod to make it die, Mrs. Brown?"

She crumbled, bawling into her hands. Everyone sat wide-eyed as the seemingly sweet little old lady gave up.

Judge Silliman raised his gavel. "Mr. and Mrs. Baker, your case is dismissed without prejudice, as it seems we have found the true culprit. Mr. Cook, your case is dismissed, without prejudice, for the same reason. Although, you might have to find a new sod vendor. Mr. Frye, the case against you is dismissed, without prejudice. You may go. Mrs. Brown, you may be sued in a civil suit for the mean thing you did to the Bakers, so be ready. It seems, after all, that the real culprit did, indeed, get what she deserved. Mr. and Mrs. Baker, you and your attorney can discuss what you want to do from here. And for crying out loud, try being nicer to your neighbors. Court adjourned."

Permed

I was just beginning to squirt the cold neutralizer on Libby's curled head when, right on the tail of, "Cover your eyes," and, "Oh, that's so cold," she blurts out, "I'm seeing someone."

"Hm?" I ask, not sure if she is hallucinating from the chemical fumes or if I've heard her wrong.

"I'm having an affair, Bev. You know, another man."

I just stare down in the taut, blue-white lines between the pink curlers; funny how that area doesn't tan… And all the time she spends at the beach I could really roll a tight curl, too; they stay in place better when they are tight. Libby usually "yows!" and I have to redo some. Such a crybaby.

"Bev! The neutralizer! You're dripping it all over the floor. Just hurry up and get it on; I think I hear my hair frizzing."

"I'm so sorry. Push that cotton up on your forehead A little, will you."

She's going to cause me to ruin this perm. I'll have this neutralizer all over her pretty little kitchen, too. Serve her right, telling me something like this.

"Libby, what are you talking about? Are you actually going... being with some guy, besides Allen?"

"Sure am." She turns and grins so smugly, like it is something to be proud of, and sits there just waiting for my next move. So, I tighten the loose curler.

"Ow!"

"Oops! Sorry."

"Oh Bev, he's wonderful. And I feel so good, better than I have in years." She tilts her head back a little so I can see her face, and how goofy she looks upside down.

"Your timing stinks, Libby. How can you tell me something like this in the middle of a perm? You're making me a nervous wreck."

"The timer! Did you set it?"

Beep, beep, beep. I set the timer for three minutes instead of five since I really have no idea how long it's been since I finished with the neutralizer." You got three minutes, Libby. Shoot."

"Sorry about just blurting it out like that. Seemed like a good time to say it. What do you think?"

I know how uncomfortable she is with toxic chemicals soaking into her skin; a translucent white drop just about to fall from her left ear lobe and probably stain her lovely oak chair if not burn a hole in the blue ruffled cushion she is sitting on. And she is waiting for me, the other half of this unconditional friendship, to give her my blessing.

"What do I think? I think you've got more energy than you know what to do with. And, I can't believe it. I can't believe you're out messing around. You're also screwing around with your life, you know."

"Bev!" Like mine, her tone somewhere between anger and disappointment.

"Okay, Libby, tell me about him. Everything." As I speak, I turn off the bright light over the large oak table; the sun is streaming in the window through the white Priscilla's, forming dust rainbows between us. I settle into the chair opposite Libby and prop my feet on another.

"He's too good. You don't want details, do you, for chrissake?"

"No. What I want to know is, I guess, why'd you let it happen, and what about Allen? He doesn't know, does he?"

"Of course not," she jumps in, a little irritably; chemicals are running into her ears, forcing her to bend sideways. She grabs a dry washcloth, wraps it around her manicured finger and sticks it in her ear.

"Well, you will have to tell him eventually. You think he can crunch numbers now, wait till you file for divorce."

I blink back an image of the usually soft-spoken Allen throwing oversized numbers at Libby as she flees the house into the arms of her faceless lover.

"Look Beverly, Allen is not going to find out. I have no intention of telling anyone but you. And there isn't going to be a divorce. I'm just incredibly bored, Bev. Allen is okay. He's a good guy, but he's boring as hell. The only time I have any fun around him is when we are with other people, like you and Paul. You know, I read an article in Reader's Digest last month that said that fun is what keeps us going. Well, until now, I haven't been going anywhere. Know what I mean?"

The buzzer screamed at us. "Let's rinse," I said, glad to have her head soaking underwater for a few minutes.

Well here we are, friends, confidants, and I'm letting her down. I'm supposed to be there for her like she was for me when I thought Paul might be having his own little fling a few years ago. But, how can I be happy for her and still look Allen in the eye over the canasta cards on Friday nights? Libby, nice name. Doesn't sound much like the name of an adulterous. Hm, what does? Victoria? Tammy? Candy? Bev?

I fix us both a Diet Coke while she is rinsing, and nibble on a piece of ice while watching her. Okay. I can admit that I'm afraid of losing a good friend to a red-hot lover; but, this is still so stupid of her.

I can just see her in her little love nest after Allen chases her from her perfect country blue home. She smiles as she invites me into the sparsely decorated one-bedroom apartment, still so much in lust that she doesn't notice the roach community on the table where she serves me tea in a Mason jar.

I lean over close to her ear and yell, "How long have you known this person?"

"Two weeks, almost."

The back door opens, admitting a miniature Libby, her dark sweaty hair in pigtails, her chubby cheeks rosy from play." Aunt Bev'ly, Paulie messed up." I untangle Jessica's jump rope, she gives me a sweaty kiss, and skips out the door. Such a charmer.

Two weeks. My, my. Wonder if they keep the lights on; she's always been so self-conscious of her stretch marks. Looks like she has lost a little weight, too. Probably been exercising more than our weekly bike ride along the beach.

She spins around with the towel turban on her curlers and a question on her face, feigning a look of innocence." Do you think I'm awful?"

"Of course I don't. It's just difficult thinking of you like this. It's gonna be different."

"Not so different as you might think."

"So, do I know him?"

"No. I met him in Calabash when I went there to shop. You know, the day you took little Paulie to the doctor. We struck up a conversation by the conch shells and ended up buying matching T-shirts, and that was just about that."

"That was that! It can't be that easy. Did one of you actually asked the other, 'hey, you want to do it?' It can't be that easy to start an affair that could set your whole world off course."

I wrap the plastic bag around her head as she laughs at my impression, set the timer again, and plunk down in a chair opposite her, looking her straight in the eye. "Have you read the paper in the last few years? Does the word AIDS ring a bell? Geez? You even wrote an article about AIDS for the Record."

"It wasn't the Record. But, no need to worry. He wears a *raincoat*," she half laughs.

It is all so clear, now. I see the two of them standing by the conch shells, she in black spandex pants and oversized hot pink sweater; he in a heavy orange, rubber rain coat and hat and black boots with large metal buckles, protected from all the elements.

"You know what I'm talking about, don't you?"

"Of course, I do. I'm not an idiot. Do you?" Her plastic wrapped head with its various colors and protrusions is beginning to look like a bad head of cabbage.

She pauses, takes a deep breath and lowers her voice a bit. "Now don't freak out on me, okay? I'm going to tell you something that I just could never say before. This isn't my first outing, so to speak. There, I said it. It's out. I didn't get AIDS, or a divorce, and I won't this time, either."

I just about stop breathing. I guess if I could see myself in a mirror, I would look like a fool with my mouth hanging open. "When?" was all I could say, and that didn't even sound like me.

"Never mind. That's not important now. That one shouldn't have happened for lots of reasons. I was just trying to make a point."

Her blasé attitude was really getting on my nerves. Some confidant she is; she had already used up one affair and I was just finding out about it.

"You've lost all your senses. If you weren't bigger than me, I think I'd smack some sense into you."

"Whoa! What do you mean, bigger than you?"

"I can't stand to talk about this anymore. You probably didn't even find out if he brushes his teeth or takes a bath on a regular basis before you jumped in bed with him."

"It wasn't a bed, the first time," she quips as she jerks the plastic cap from her wet head."

Of course it wasn't a bed. Silly me. They were wearing nothing but their matching T-shirts while they steamed up the back room of the store, their mingling sweat soaking a new shipment of shirts. The orange raincoat close at hand.

"Well, you can take the curlers out by yourself. I've got to get home."

"I'll call you later," she yells as I finished strapping Paulie onto my Schwinn and start to pedal down the drive.

~.~

I had been pushing a heavy cart along the wet sand in North Myrtle Beach, hawking slices of pizza to sun-drenched families who didn't have the energy or desire to leave the beach in search of anything better, when I first met Libby. She was pushing a similar cart in the opposite direction, hawking not-quite-frozen lemonade. We would nod our heads, at first, and push on, jiggling those goofy bells we were required to jiggle non-stop. It wasn't a bad summer job for someone not really into work but needed the money to support a car. Didn't matter what I wore, so I'd grease down my body and wear a bathing suit most days. Had a dynamite tan.

It was a slow day, I was passing by two kids, both about eight or so, who were doing a darn good job of molding a shark in the sand. I couldn't help but make a few artistic suggestions, and then the urge to squat down to form my own work of art was absolutely overwhelming.

"Hey, Michelangelo, you're gonna get your butt fired." Hanging over my shoulder was the not-quite-frozen lemonade girl, my soon to be best friend for life, Libby.

"Nobody wants pizza today, anyway. Too hot out here. How you doing?"

"Good. It's hotter than hell out here. Good day for lemonade."

She was introducing herself while checking out my sand work. I was finishing up as she handed me a lemonade and began pushing her cart.

"See you at the end of the line," mingled with the jiggling bell as she pushed on down the beach.

I ran into Libby again that very night. I was floating in the pool of the Dunes Hotel; the bigger the hotel the less likely anyone was to notice that we weren't paying guests.

"How's the water, Michelangelo?"

Again, I look over my shoulder to see the lemonade girl.

"The water is great. Haven't seen you around here before."

"I just found out where everybody goes after work. Besides, I haven't been around here long. Did you finish your octopus?"

"Sure. Even sold a few pepperoni slices before I called it quits."

She had thick dark hair that hung down to the middle of her back and round eyes just as dark. Looking past her I could see a couple of bums checking out the contents of her small bikini. Following my gaze, she smiled, flipped her mane over her right shoulder and slid into the water.

She cocked her head in their direction. "Are those guys as available as they look?"

"Probably. Hard to tell if they are sweating or slobbering, isn't it, but they seem okay."

"Okay? Do you need some glasses, girl?" They look like they fell off a cover of Playgirl magazine."

We started hanging out together a lot after work, and really could have a lot of fun, on the nights when she wasn't tracing the ripples on yet another tanned hunk. Wherever we were, we would watch people around us, anticipate their moves, make up lewd and licentious details about their lives, and often laughed till it hurt when one of our victims made a move that seemed to validate what we had guessed. But, I never totally understood my new friend.

"Libby, what's with you? Can't you be satisfied with one guy for the summer?"

"Aw Bev, you're just a little jealous. I'll share with you." She giggled at the roll of my eyes. "You know what you are, Bev? You're the last virgin in the world."

~.~

I guess I shouldn't be so surprised to find that Libby hasn't been the faithful wife, but I really did think that marriage had made a difference, even for her. There is no getting around the fact that we lead a boring life around here. Never anything new. I feel the urge for a serious talk with my hubby about our very un-social life. I'll hit him when his belly is full and happy.

"Hey babe," I say in that husky sexy voice that he likes, while massaging the soles of his feet with my toes; not an easy task since I have to extend my leg from the couch to the recliner where he has taken root. "I've been thinking about something."

"Oh God. Look out," is his jerky reply. I wonder if he really thinks he is being clever. I wonder if he would ever say that again if he knew the things I consider doing to him every time he does that? But, I just smile; I'm on a mission.

"Come on, I'm serious," I coo as I run my toes up his pant leg. "We really need to get involved in something new; you must be bored sitting in front of that television all the time. We just don't really do anything that is fun anymore, and I'm kinda tired of playing canasta every single Friday night of my life."

"What do you want to do?" His face still enveloped in Field and Stream.

I snicker at the image of a catfish with a death grip on Paul's nose. A real attention getter.

"I want to do something different. Something fun." I ran off my list of possibilities as my own excitement began to build. "You know what I'd really love to do?"

"What?" asked the talking magazine.

"The two-step. I'd really like to take dance lessons. Wouldn't that be neat?"

"Bev, you know I don't like to dance. I just don't think all that physical stuff is fun after working all week. We do other stuff now and then, like see a play."

"I suppose you know," I inform him, in a not-so-sweet voice, and removing my toes from his pants leg, "that we haven't been to a play together in about three years. And would you mind looking at me when we talk!"

Well, he lowers that paper and looks at me in his "What else do you want to say?" look, and I decide I don't want to say another thing to this man on this night. I was feeling flushed and a little nauseous, reeling in the realization that we had had so many similar conversations that went nowhere for over ten years. I felt too tired to pursue this tonight. I checked on Paulie; such a sweet little boy; the joy of my life. He was building garages for his little cars.

It was right about then that the phone rang. Before today, I would complain to Libby, and she would echo something similar about her love-twinkie. Now, she probably doesn't care what Allen is doing. Probably saving her energy for Mr. Calabash.

"Bev, can we talk? You can't really be mad at me can you? I can't get the image of your disappointed look out of my mind."

"What do I have to be mad about?" Still feeling the sting of the sweet-nothings exchanged between Paul and myself.

"I knew you couldn't stay mad at me. We're just too great of friends to be on the outs, especially over a guy. You know what would be nice for tomorrow? We could go to Garden City early, have breakfast, lay on the beach a while. All those Spring break crazies aren't down there. Whatcha think, Bevie?"

Paul drifts by with his new fishing rod.

I can see him standing waist deep in foaming waves, casting his line out farther than he's ever cast before. He jerks forward, then reflexes back before he lunges face down into the water, riding the crests into the horizon. I didn't even know he could body surf.

"What the heck. Might as well go to the beach. Maybe get a tattoo." We both laugh at that, a long-standing pact to not mar our bodies.

"We haven't been to the beach together all week. It'll be great. Maybe rent some jet skis."

"Hey Lib, do you know of anywhere around here to learn belly-dance? I've heard it is a great way to self-bond."

"Oooh. I like it."

It was beginning to feel right again. "I've been thinking," as I catch my reflection in the microwave door, "What do you think about Highlighting my hair? I need a change."

Crossing Over

Hey, you old bag-of-bones. What's up?" Rocky had been one of the first of the residents out tonight, enjoying the brisk coolness of the night air and the full moon that cast light and shadows, creating an outline of a cityscape in blacks and grays that didn't exist. He dangled his feet in the icy water of the slow-moving stream. The colorless leaves that floated by in the moonlight would be bright oranges, yellows and reds in the light of day.

The Counselor eased himself down next to Rocky and returned his insult with a handful of grass in his face. "How's that nose of yours? Still hanging on?"

"Yep, still there. I'd sure miss it if it weren't. You know, the women loved it, back in the day. They thought it was sort of sexy. Like, maybe, a guy with a crooked nose was a tough guy. Anyways, never had any complaints." Rocky reached for his nose as if checking that it was, indeed, still attached.

Counselor chuckled. "You have a lot of interesting stories, Rocky." He took a few moments to take in the beauty of the sky that surrounded the moon. "Sure is a glorious night."

Rocky leaned over to remove a slimy leaf that had hung on to his foot.

"Got anything you want to talk about tonight, Rocky?" Counselor asked.

"Nope. Nothing comes to mind, right now. If I tell you everything all at once, you might think I'm a terrible person. I'll just ease some of my wickedness out a bit at a time, if that's all right with you? I'm not in much of a hurry, anyways. It's sort of nice here. Don't think I ever felt this relaxed in my whole life."

"Sure, Rocky. You know I got all the time in the world."

"How about you?" asked Rocky. "You got anything to talk about? You need to get some junk off your chest, too, dontcha?"

"I'm okay. Don't be worrying about this old-bag-of-bones."

Rocky looked around at the others who sat on benches or walked the grounds, whispering to themselves or someone else. "Looks like there are some new folks around here. Guess I missed a lot when I didn't come out for a while. What's up?"

"Well, there's a nice elderly couple over there. Came in together yesterday. Car wreck. I'm leaving them to themselves for a while. They've been huddled together since they've been here. Sort of in shock, and they have a lot to work through from all their years together."

"Really?" Rocky was surprised. "I'd think if you lived together that long you've said about all there is to say. But I guess you know more about that than me."

"Ever been married, Rocky?"

"That's not a good story. Didn't last long. She was a bubble-gum chewing, cussin' and drinking kind of woman. I sort of liked it at first, but then it got old. But, hey, what about that grouchy old geezer that came in a while back?"

"Got any kids to talk about?" Counselor ignored Rocky's attempt to change the direction of the conversation.

"Not that I know of. You know something I don't?"

"No, just messing with you, Rocky. The 'old geezer' is George. I hear him mumbling in there. Don't sound none too happy about anything. We'll know more, later."

"I saw a snake wriggling in the water before you came out. Wonder how many are in there? Hope there's none of them where I'm going." Rocky shook at the thought of snakes in his future.

"Well, you can use your time counting them, or you can tell me more about your interesting life as a boxer."

"All right. Ain't much to tell. I started boxing early at a neighborhood gym. They were just keeping us hoodlums off the streets. I took to it right away. I had a whole lot of mad in me, so punching a bag, and then other boys' faces, suited me just fine."

"And, I did pretty good, won a lot of fights. I went to Vegas for some matches. Met some sweet women out there. That was a different kind of life than the little town I grew up in. I learned some stuff I never needed to know."

"I learned enough to get into some trouble now and again. You know, bet on the matches. I even threw a few. Hated that but the big boss said I had to. You don't mess with the big boss or you might lose your eyeballs. That's about it, Counselor."

"Like I told you, Rocky. I got all the time in the world. And, keep in mind, there's more than One Big Boss to answer to, and you could lose something bigger than your eyes. Later, though."

Rocky cocked his head like he was studying the Counselor. "You already know everything, don't you?"

Counselor smiled. "Later, Rocky."

~*~

"Is this all ya'll ever do around here, yak, yak? It's hard to think my own thoughts with all the racket," complained the newcomer.

"Look at those duds he's wearing. That's some money there," whispered Rocky.

"Been waiting for you to show up, George. You've been hiding out quite a while. Want to join us?"

"How you know my name? Have we met?" George kept his hands pushed into his pockets.

"Hi. I'm Rocky. We saw your name when you came in. Nice suit you're wearing."

"Yeah. It's the only thing my no-count wife did that I asked her to do. Guess it didn't fit her new boyfriend. It won't matter much, either, if I sit on the ground here. Who cares if I get dirty. She sure won't."

"Sounds like you brought a lot of anger with you, George. Wanna talk about it?"

"Ah, you're the one. I heard I was supposed to tell my story to someone, I guess you're the Counselor guy? What the heck does it matter if I tell you the whole ugly story? It won't change nothing. She promised to do everything I asked her to do, but she was just a selfish...well, you know."

"You're really angry with your wife?"

"Sure I am. You would be to. I had the money to do it all. But she was a greedy wench. She wanted every dime I had. I know she had a guy, then, too. She was acting funny and dressing up more than usual. If I could do it, right now, I'd plum wring her neck." His mouth managed a wicked-looking sneer. "I'd wring his, too."

That last sentence made Rocky a bit uneasy. "Um, I think I'll let you two talk. I'll just mosey around and check out the new folks," he said. He ambled off into the shadows.

"Are you saying that you would actually kill your wife if you had the chance? That's pretty harsh, isn't it?"

"Listen, buddy. She cuckolded me. She double-crossed me big time, when I trusted her with my life. I had it all arranged and paid for and she took the money. That much I know, because look where I am. She used a miserably small bit of my money to get me here. Yes, I'm full of hate. If I could get hold of the right people from wherever I am now, it would get done. I deserve to hate her."

George continued. "You know what my big dream was? If I ever got real sick, I'd be frozen until there was a cure. I'm an intelligent man, a good brain. I could've made a difference in a later life. She killed me, let me die like a fool."

George hung his head. His suit was sagging around his shoulders. It was hard to tell whether sadness or anger held him up. But his anger was intense and would need some time to resolve, if possible. Some folks just don't want to let go of the very thing that leaves them in misery.

"Maybe we can talk some more tomorrow night, George. You seem tuckered out."

"I am tired. Been through a lot. It's her fault, and that boyfriend of hers. I figured out who he was. She couldn't fool me. I had too many connections. I don't think it will matter how much we talk, Mr. Counselor. I hate that woman with everything I got, though I ain't got much now."

He slowly got up to leave, mumbling obscenities.

~*~

Counselor waited while the icy water rushed across the bones of his feet. He waited for Rocky, knowing he would return. About the same time that George's mumbling faded away, Rocky was sliding back to the creek's edge.

"Boy oh boy. He is one mad old coot, isn't he?"

"Do you think maybe he has a right to feel wronged?"

There was a long silence. Only hushed whisperings from around the grounds as some residents made peace and others held on to their evil feelings. It was all a matter of time before they decided which way they wanted to go. The Counselor could only do so much. He never was, never would be, a miracle worker.

"So, I want to get this straight." Rocky turned to face counselor. "I've been here a long time.I have to tell my whole story to make peace, is that right?"

"Sort of," responded Counselor. "You have to make peace with yourself and your past, the best you can. Or, you can go on holding on to all that bad stuff. Your choice."

"I felt bad about that guy, George. He was sort of scary, too. I bet he made his wife miserable, is why she did what she did."

"How does that have anything to do with you, Rocky?"

"I did a lot of bad things in my life. I told you almost all that I remember. But most of the time, I was a pretty cool guy. I was real close to my older sister. She tried to raise me right. Poor girl, had to bury me, too. But I tell you, she sure did that right. I helped people out when I could, know what I mean? Never hurt anyone on purpose.

"Hm."

"Well, I want to be totally honest with you, Counselor. With myself, too." As Rocky continued to talk, a soft aura circled him from head to toe. His voice grew softer, slowly fading.

"It was me that had an affair with George's wife. I feel real bad about it. I'm not the one that killed him, though. Honest. But that's someone else's story, right?"

Counselor nodded.

"Even when he was talking about killing me, I couldn't hate him. I was his wife's lover. I felt sorry for her. Wanted to protect her because she told me how mean he was, and all. I wish it had never happened. I wish he was able to get frozen like he wanted. I'm sorry for everything about it. Had no idea it would get so crazy. You know, with all his connections and money, nobody cared when he died. Now, that's the worst lonely I can imagine. You've seen my stone, haven't you, Counselor? I knew my sister cared, but didn't expect her to go all out like she did. That's real love."

Rocky's last words could barely be heard, they were so soft and distant. He had finished his story. He was finally at peace and ready to move on.

Counselor walked over to Rocky's grave site and admired the love of a sister that would use all the money she had to have two bronze boxing gloves placed on her brother's stone.

He rested against the large tree that cast shadows on both Rocky and George's plots and whose roots grew as deep as the secrets in stories yet untold.

His thoughts moved to George, his anger and disappointments. "He's going to take a lot of time. But, hey, that's what I've got a lot of."

<u>Rebirth</u>

Jake had just wiped down the bar. His bones ached after a long night on his feet, listening to drunken stories by the regulars, and blasted from all sides by raucous music from a local rock band. His ears hurt. His head ached. The phone in his pocket buzzed...an unknown number. He ignored it. He did the same again the second and third time. His philosophy...*if you can't leave a freaking message, it's not important enough for me to answer.*

He was especially tired this week after covering extra hours for the owner who tended the bar occasionally. Jake generally liked tending bar, not a lot of thinking to it. He'd lived a rough-ass year, and thinking was not a favorite pastime.

On the way home, the phone rang two more times. He stepped on the gas pedal a little harder. He took a deep breath and let up on the gas. "Don't be stupid Jake-o." He slowed to a little over the speed limit. January rain is cold, slick and black...not a time for driving mad. Jake felt a dark heaviness fall over him, as he thought of Amanda and Lily on a similar night, a little over a year ago. He held the guilt like glass in his gut. "I should have been there." Tears ran down his face. He felt his jaw tighten. He wondered how long it would take for the pain to lessen. Some days weren't as bad as others. The best he could do.

The second call played the tune of Superman. "Hey, Jake. Just checking in with you, hadn't heard from you today.'

"Yeah. Sorry about that Mike. I'm working extra hours this week. I told you I was gonna do that, right?"

"You did. But, you know what we say."

"Yep. *Don't get too tired, too hungry or too lonely*. I appreciate you making sure I never get lonely." He allowed a tired chuckle at his own humor.

"You get the smart-ass blue ribbon, buddy. Talk tomorrow." The phone went quiet.

Jake did appreciate the hell out of Mike, who pretty much saved him from his own sorry self this past year. He was always at the other end of a phone call, no matter the time or situation. Mike wasn't ever happy about the situation, and never let Jake get away with anything. That's what made him a great friend, and an even better AA sponsor.

~.~

At home, Jake threw his car keys on the counter and his leather jacket in the direction of the only chair in the living room, but missed. He rolled some deli turkey with Colby cheese and called it supper, and ate while he checked the mail. He finished in all of three seconds with the pile of junk-mail and pitched it in the trash. "Crap, gotta get some mouse traps," he mumbled, as he picked up mouse droppings with a paper towel. He really hated seeing them on the kitchen counter. He showered quickly and slid into bed naked, still damp. Too tired to care, and headed into a fitful sleep, full of nightmares. Nothing unusual.

His dreams often included motorcycles, blood, screams and a bridge. Sometimes he heard his baby crying, and this is what often woke him in the middle of the night, only to find he was the one crying.

He heard a distant sound, but was not awake enough to identify it. It became more annoying when he realized it was his phone. The ringing stopped. The pleasant aroma of coffee seeped into his bedroom. The clock blinked 7 a.m., and he remembered he had set his alarm for an important meeting. He was ready to start his life over, to finally get on with it. To do something worthwhile. The ringing started again.

The number was still unfamiliar, but the same one as last night. He pulled on a clean pair of jeans and made his way to the coffee. "If the damn thing rings again…." And it did.

"What?"

"Hi Jake. Do you know who this is?" The voice on the other end shared an irritating hint of timidity and cheer.

"Is this a contest, lady? I'm in no mood for twenty questions."

"Jake, I hope your mood improves, for Christ sake. Amanda. It's Amanda."

Jake gripped the counter. "What the hell? Who...?"

"It's really me, Jake. Honest. Me and Lily are okay. I felt so guilty. I couldn't let it go on any longer. I miss you. It was all Momma's doing. Please forgive me."

He pressed the end-call button *and* stared at the phone. His thoughts raced. *She's alive. Lily is alive. My baby girl.* The phone rang, again. "Let me talk to her."

"She doesn't know you. We need to give it time. She isn't here right now, anyway."

"How can this...what the crap did you do? You were dead. My daughter was dead. Are you telling me that you and your whole damned family played a cruel joke on me? You wanted out? What the hell?"

His chest hurt like hell, pressure…anger for her and her whole hillbilly-ass family…joy that his child was alive, not dust in the wind. A whole year of grieving and crying, hating and loneliness.

"How could you do that Amanda? I want my child. What am I supposed to do about this? Shit, shit, shit." He held his hand after banging it on the counter.

"It was a mistake. I want us to be a family, Jake. I really do."

"You're effing right about the mistake. You might not know how big a mistake. If I could get hold of you right now…"

"Please, Jake. I shouldn't have listened to Mom, she kept pushing me to do it. You were drinking and using again, and…"

"What? What the hell? You were, too."

"No. I wanted to get clean. And you took off after we had that stupid fight. I didn't know where you were, whether you'd come back. Mom said she would take care of everything. That she would find you and tell you that we were in a wreck, and were cremated and all that. I didn't even know, at first, that she told you we both were dead. I felt so awful about it."

"IT? You felt awful about IT? I'm not even believing this. IT was just done? Do you have any idea what IT did to me? I tried to kill myself. I'd never had so much pain in my life. You crazy bitch. What were you thinking?"

Jake was screaming and crying, wiping his face with the backs of his hands. "I could wring your neck right now. I just want to hear it crack." His hands shook. He braced himself against the counter.

"No, Jake. Listen, we need to talk, for our daughter. She needs you, too."

"You're crazy. How could you do this to me, to Lily? How could anyone do this? Where are you, dammit?"

The line went dead, but he held the phone in his hand. He felt wobbly, drunk. "What just happened?" he screamed. He could hear his words echoing in his head. He grabbed a lamp and threw it across the room where it hit the wall and dragged the skimpy curtain down with it as it crashed to the floor. He kicked the closet door that had been hanging open for weeks, shattering slats that left a gaping hole.

Someone was banging on his door. "Jake, Open up. What's going on in there?"

Jake unlocked the door and walked away without opening it. Mike, who lived downstairs pushed the door open, and cautiously looked in. "What happened here, man?"

Jake collapsed on the couch.

Mike poured two cups of coffee. He listened and shook his head as Jake cried, cursed, and told the whole ugly story of what a mess he used to be and the fake deaths of his girlfriend and his baby. He laughed, "Today, man. You know what today was supposed to be for me? I can't believe... it's too much. Today was supposed to be my new beginning. I was making plans to get on with my life, to start college. Shit. That's what my life is...always will be."

"Did you love her then, Amanda?"

"We were both shit-faced. Who knows? We were….are…damaged goods. Only good thing to come from us was a beautiful little baby. Dammit, she's probably walking now." He screamed into a pile of unfolded clothes on the couch. "Know what she had the nerve to say? Huh? Said Lily doesn't know me. Like that's my fault." He kicked the arm of the couch. "Aw crap." He held his foot with both hands. "Broke a freaking toe."

"Think about it, Jake. You were pretty messed up. Could you have been a good father? You needed this year."

"Are you kidding? I almost died this year. I was grieving my ass off."

"You got clean and sober. You would have been dead, not a father, if you didn't go through the pain and get help."

"So, I'm supposed to be grateful for what she did to me? That's all messed up, man."

"If you want to be a good dad, you will have to focus on your little girl, not her lying mother. Think about it."

"I can't. I want her and her whole crazy family to all just effing die. That's what I need. I could get my daughter and disappear. That's what I'm thinking."

~.~

It was a beautiful March day. Early blooming spring flowers and trees basked in the warm sunshine after a week of heavy rain and cold winds.

They'd only had two weeks to get to know each other. Jake held Lily close and wouldn't let anyone else come near. She was as beautiful as he had imagined she would be, a lot like her momma, but sweeter. Golden ringlets circled the little girl's face. Her blue eyes twinkled as she looked into Jake's eyes and held his face with her tiny hands.

Jake held tight to Lily, so happy that she took to him right away. *"Doesn't know me, my ass,"* he thought. He kept his eyes on the crowd that gathered. He only trusted his friend, no one else. *"They'd all probably like to stab me in my gut if they could,"* he thought. Lilly played with his mustache and giggled, which made him smile and softened his thoughts.

People stole glances and talked in hushed tones, as they usually do in a funeral home. Most of them were Amanda's family and friends. Amanda lay in a white casket with pink roses draped across. Mike sat with Jake and Lily. A policeman stood at the door. Mike had asked for security, not knowing what might happen between Jake and Amanda's family.

Jake wanted to leave. His daughter didn't understand what was happening, that her mother would never be back. This time she really was dead. But a sense of decency, that sort of pissed him off, made him see this through. When this funeral crap was just a weird memory for him, he and Lily had the rest of their lives to be happy together. He could easily visualize the life they would share. Just imagining his little girl growing and starting school made him smile.

He leaned over to Mike. "Is it okay that I am so darn happy I can hardly sit still? Does it make me a horrible person?"

Mike reached over and tickled Lily's chin. She giggled and hid her face with her dad's hand. "Just focus on your kid. You've got an opportunity here, Jake, to be the best person you can be and a reason to live."

Amanda's mother walked toward Jake and Lily. Everyone's eyes were on her. Mike walked over to the policeman and whispered his words of caution for what could become a volatile situation.

"Can I take Lily up front, to the casket to see…"

"No!"

"Can I at least hold her for a minute?" she sobbed.

"Granny. This is my daddy. Why are you crying?" The grief of one and the joy of the other broke Jake's cold resolve. He stood, still keeping Lily close to his heart.

"Just for a minute. Then we have to leave. Long ride home." He leaned closer to Amanda's mother. "Don't do anything stupid. I'm not in the mood."

~.~

Lily slept much of the way home. Mike and Jake spoke little, neither feeling the need. It had been an exhausting month of dealing with Amanda as she kept at Jake to consider forgetting what she had done so they could all be a happy family.

She played her senseless games of not showing up when they were supposed to meet, and threatened to have him arrested for desertion, among other things. Jake gained the upper hand when he asked her pastor to intercede...hard to believe she actually did go to church. Another thing her mother prodded her to do.

Then the next two weeks were loaded with ups and downs. Jake got a room at a hotel near Amanda's house so it would be easy to see Lily every day. What he suspected was true...Amanda's most recent lover dumped her, so she decided it was time to contact him and reunite.

She showed up at the hotel, uninvited. She was angry that Jake had no interest in playing house with her. She smelled of bourbon, and wanted to take Lily. Jake stepped out in the hall so that Lily wouldn't hear them. She was listening to children's songs on his iPod. "If you don't want to be a part of our family, you might as well go back to where you came from," said Amanda. Me and Lily don't need nothing from you." She drew her hand back to slap him in the face, but he caught her wrist and held tight.

"You get out of here. This is my time with my child. I never want you in my face again. Understand?"

"Good riddance. I can do better than you anyhow." She stumbled down the hall to the elevator. It was after the elevator doors closed that it occurred to him that she was wearing chaps. "*Stupid bitch*," he thought.

~,~

"Hey, Jake. Let me take the wheel for a while. You've got to be wore out."

"I am. I'll get a little shut-eye, if I can." He looked at Lily resting in her car seat. It made him breathe easier just to look at her."

Before he fell asleep, a slew of thoughts tunneled their way into his semi-consciousness. Jake remembered that he had always told Amanda she couldn't handle a motorcycle on a wet road. The girl never listened to anybody.

But, his last thoughts, before drifting off to a peaceful sleep, were of Lily's tiny hands, like chubby stars on his cheeks, a sensation of joy, and a heavy burden lifted from him.

The Ravines of Bell County

"That, boy, is what pure stupid looks like." That's the way Pops would speak. He kept things straightforward and simple, black and white. He wasn't one to talk a lot. He usually saved his words for somethin important, which was usually business or family. So, I guessed that day was an opportunity to teach me somethin important.

We'd been sittin at the supper table, just passin Mama's buttery, finger-lickin cornbread around the table when we heard, BOOM! I swear, it shook the ground right under us. There's that funny space when we was all big-eyed, lookin around to see if everyone was still there, hopin it wasn't the rapture, cause you done did something you know, for sure, you shouldn't.

As soon as we ran outside, we saw the big plume of smoke over the trees, comin directly from our closest neighbor's house. Pops and Mama jumped in the cab of the pickup, barely waitin for me and Annie to climb over the tailgate and into the back. We were at Bo's place in a few minutes, or so.

And there I stood, next to Pops. My eyes were hot from the heat of the fire. I felt like I had concrete in my legs. I couldn't make'm move backwards, away from the heat. So, there I stood. Starin. Those flames roared and stretched high into the sky, and burned into a place in my brain that ain't never left. We got there too late to hear poor ole Bo Bodin's last screams. I'm glad of that. His house, more like an overgrown shack, was engulfed in flames. Rollin clouds of gray smoke blocked out the sunset, which would'a looked right pretty from behind poor ole Bo's place. That is, if it weren't burned down to the ground. No chance of savin him or any part of that house. He was dead. No doubt about it.

All our neighbors were there. I knew 'em all. You don't live in a small community like ours and have strangers in your midst, not for long, anyway. The menfolk started forming groups near the trucks. The women moved away from the house, into the shade of some big oak trees. Some of the little kids, who had no grasp about what just happened, were running around playing catchers and laughin. I was prone to listenin to the menfolk. That's what I did a lot of, listen and watch. My Pops said that was a good habit to acquire, especially in the hills of Bell County.

The men were shakin their heads. Some lit pipes while most chewed and spit, formin their own personal puddles of floatin tobacca flakes. I figured I'd probably smoke a pipe when I'm old enough. There's something sorta mezmerizin about the lightin of a pipe. Then the menfolk commenced to workin the situation out.

"Bo jist would'n listen to nobody."

"Had to do it some idjit way."

"I told him once, and only once, that he was gonna kill hisself." That was Pops. Like I said, he don't waste words, especially on a idjit.

"Thought he was puttin somethin over on the revenooers. Thought he could put that still right in the middle of his house, and they'd never look there."

"Twern't for those revenooers and that darn probition, Bo wouldn't be scorched now."

"And they darn tootin won't look there, now, will they?" Some of 'em snickered and snorted. No time for tomfoolery in the hills. You live smart, or you die.

"Well, nuthin to do, here, right now. He got any kin?"

"We should wait 'bout a week or so to push it all into the ravine, back there. Make certain ain't nothing still burnin."

"Seems a shame, but I guess we'll have to wait till tomorrow to look for any remains of Bo."

"Yep."

They mumbled around a little, so I moseyed on over to study what was left of Bo's home, which collapsed into itself, just smokin wood, mostly. Sort of weird, standin right in front of the charred remains of a human bein, his house and his blowed up still. I ain't never seen anythin like it in my whole life, up to that point. The funny thing, sorta, about these hills, it's so quiet. You hear nothin, and you hear everthin. Most time you can hear the animals breathin in the barn. Poor ole Bo mighta rotted here fore anyone knew he was dead if he hadn't died so noisy. Be a long time before I'd forget about the day Bo Bodin died.

So we went on home and finished our meal, which wasn't hot no more. Nobody talked. Just ate. Before we left the table, Pops read a passage from his Bible. I barely heard'im. I was wonderin how long the charred smell was gonna stay in my nose.

***

Pops wanted me to learn to be a businessman. So, I pretty much got to run the vegetable stand at the end of our road on my own. That's a real responsible position for a twelve-year-old. Pops didn't seem to care much if I sold a lot or a little. We would eat what didn't sell, before it got too ripe. The corn grew behind my stand until it was ready to harvest. Then I sold corn. Not all of it...Pops kept a lot to hisself for his other business.

Annie helped Mama in the big garden at the side of the house. I did too, when she needed me. Everyone worked. No laziness around Pops. A person had to earn the right to play or relax. Just the way it was.

Pops reminded me pert near ever day, or so, that part of my work was to keep my eyes and ears wide open. "Don't miss anythin unusual, boy. A strange car, men in suits. It could be a matter of life or death for someone."

So I did. Watched and listened all the time. Life and death stuff is scary, and I ain't gonna be the one to be on the wrong side of it. Ever now and again, I would leave my stand and find Pops to alert him of somethin out of the ordinary. Pops would rub my head and said "Good job, Eugene." Then he would grab his rifle off the wall just inside the door, over the bookshelf where his Bible rested. And in no time flat, his truck was skiddin down the dirt road, sendin dogs an chickens scatterin.

~.~

It was a cool Sunday mornin in the hills. I watched the sunrise with Pops, Mama and Annie on the back porch. Mama had cooked up a batch of eggs, grits and biscuits. Boy, could I slather the butter and Mama's blackberry preserves on my steamy biscuits. Yup, I'd rather had this meal more'n anything from some fancy restaurant in the city. I put my eggs on top of a thick, juicy slice of tomato from Mama's garden. Sometimes she would think about it and hand me my plate with that tomato already sliced and under my eggs. No better way to start the day. No way on earth.

Today we go to church. Mama couldn't get Pops to go more'n once a month, so that's when we went. I remember her sayin, "We go as a family, or we don't go." She could be stern as a rock when she wanted. I don't think Pops wanted to go at all, but Mama told him that he didn't want to be responsible for us children losin our chance at salvation. I guess that moved his heart some.

Me and Annie sure liked church. We liked singin loud. "The louder you sung, the more you praised the Lord," Moma told us. After services, there was a picnic. Yummy dishes full of all the women-folk's best recipes loaded the tables under a stand of trees in the back of the Pentecostal Church.

Us boys would climb trees and wrestle around. Now and again a scuffle would be broke up by someone's mama, but most of the time we scuffled till we were done.

The menfolk played horseshoes, whittled, or just huddled for talk that no one else was to hear. I'd been practicing a long time behind our barn, just waitin for the day I'd join in. "It's just a game, boy. You still have some growin to do to become a man."

Before the sun set over the trees behind the Pentecostal Church, we were in our truck, headed for home. Tired, but happy. I looked at a nasty scrape on my knee, needed some soap and water, but didn't hurt much. Annie whined about being tired, so she got to sit up front with Mama. I didn't mind, though. I liked bein to myself.

Mama and Pops were talkin and smiling up there in the cab, I liked to see them do that. Most of the time everybody's so darn serious around here. Yep, that was one of the happiest days in my life. Only way it could be better would be some more hot biscuits before I went to bed.

The morning after church-Sunday was real cool again, but started getting real hot about noon. The sun was blastin right over my head as I tended the vegetable stand. There was always more traffic when time came to sell Mama's preserves. Mama cooked up so many berries I could sell 'em all year round. People love 'em.

Pops left early in the mornin to go to town. Didn't ask anyone if they might want to go. I would'a liked to, but I don't impose myself on Pops. He knows I would'a gone if he asked. So I rearranged my stand now and again, knocking off dust from the cars goin by, which wasn't all that much.

An old green Chevy pulled to the side of the road and stopped. As the door opened I waved. "Mornin Pastor McCoy. Can I help you?"

"I know you can. Howyadoin this fine day, Eugene?"

"Just fine, Pastor. And, you?" I was nervous around the Pastor. Felt like he was lookin right through me. I ain't never been a real bad kid, but I don't know exactly how to measure a little bad and a lot bad. I know the Pastor does, though. I just work at bein as proper as I know how when I see him.

"This is clearly a day the Lord hath made, Eugene. Beautiful. So, you know I surely want some of those preserves. Don't know what she does, but your momma works some magic there. Two tomatoes, one onion, and a green pepper. What do I owe ya?"

Before he headed down the road, Pastor McCoy rubbed my hair, blessed me and left me a dime tip. I bit into a juicy tomato and was wonderin what it must be like to be responsible for so many souls. Must be tough work around these parts.

I pitched the tomato and wiped juice from my face when I heard another engine down the road a piece. It was a gray sedan, sorta new. I wasn't so good with newer cars, but I could tell you the make and model of ever truck in the hills around us. And not one was as new as this car. The paint was still shinin and the tread of the tires was deep.

He took his time getting out of the car, fiddling with papers in a notebook. A short, stocky man got out. He had a bulge under his jacket. A gun. City guy. No beard. Clean car. I didn't like him from the get-go.

I waited. He spoke first. "Howdy, young man. How's business?"

"Fair enough."

"Looks good. I'll take a couple'a tomatoes." He had his hands on his hips lookin around. "You live down this road, here?"

"I do."

"Your daddy home?"

"Nope."

"Anybody home?"

"What you need to know for, mister?"

"I just want to talk to your daddy, maybe look around. Thinking about buying some property up here. How much land your daddy have?"

"I done told ya he's not here. Ain't no one here ya need to talk to. And there's no land for sale. Here's your stuff." He paid up, pitched his bag into the front seat of his car, and turned around again. He was walkin towards the road to our house. I moved quickly from behind the stand and stood in front of him.

"Your business here is over, mister. Like I said, there ain't nobody here for ya to talk to. Ya got a phone number or address, ya can leave that with me."

"You're a tough one, aren't ya. I'll probably be comin around here in ten years lookin you up." He smiled and I liked him even less. I watched till the rear of his car disappeared 'round the bend. Then I high-tailed it to the house.

I was out of breath and my heart was thumpin in my throat. But Mama got the message. She grabbed her rifle off the wall, where it hung with Pop's. I grabbed Pops' gun, and Mama nodded. "Let's git."

Mama was not a prissy woman, and she knew how to use a rifle almost as good as Pops. But I never knew she could run so fast. I was gaspin for air followin her through rough brush. She ran as fast as she could go. A deer spooked just ahead of us, kicked up his hind legs and skeedaddled. I had followed Pops through these woods before. He went a different way each time. Now Mama was takin another. I was wishin there weren't so many stickers.

I could hear her breathin heavy, over my own breathin. Now and again Mama would yell out another question about this stranger, and I would struggle and push out the answer. Her fierce determination to get there before him scared me a lot. I was wonderin what we would find when we got there. Hopin Pops would already be there ahead of us to sort things through. I didn't like the way this day was fleshin out.

We broke through the brush and the familiar scene of Pops' stills, the shed, and the wall. Pops had explained it all to me some years back. It didn't seem so scary then. Mama readied the rifle and looked around. There was nothin to do but wait.

Mama told me, by noddin, to get behind the wall. Pops had told me it was for protection in case any bad cowboys or injuns were shootin at me. I looked it over for the first time. Made of wood and heavy metal. Maybe bullet-proof. Surely arrow-proof. It was camouflaged with the same sticker brush that had scratched and torn at my skin and clothes. I looked at Mama's face. It was a face I wasn't used to seein. Tight lips. Eagle eyes, searchin, waitin. Muscles in her jaw twitched. I'd seen Pops jaw look like that before, when he was mad or just really serious 'bout somethin.

I surveyed the circle of land that surrounded the stills, the shack and this wall, that was supposed to be hidden deep in the hills. I'd been payin attention since I was in diapers. There were others out there - circles of land, hidin things that weren't nobody's business but the owners.

The trees and brush were thick. Good for hidin in, and good for sneakin up on, too. Mama jerked her head, listenin. She heard something, for sure. I might've, but not certain. "Keep down boy. Don't know what will happen next."

"I have a rifle, too, Mama."

She smiled at me, real proud like, and her face softened, like I'm used to. "You're a good boy, Eugene. You'll be a good, strong man." Then she turned back to the business of waitin.

We both eyed him at the same time. I could feel Mama tense just as I did. He was almost directly across from us, but he couldn't see us. Not yet. We watched as he looked around, cautiously movin closer in, his revolver in his right hand. My heart was thuddin so hard, it hurt. I was fightin back tears...don't know why they were tryin to come out, 'cept I was scared near to death. I had to be a man today, for Mama.

The stranger backed up to the trees again, keepin a watch out as he went. He came back with an ax. He was at least a little stupid, 'cause he tucked his revolver in behind his pants belt. I guess when Mama yelled at him, he knew it would be a bad move to, right away, reach for it. You know, like in the Westerns at the movies, where if ya draw for your gun, it's automatically a gunfight.

"You're close enough, mister. You're on private property and I'm tellin ya to get off my land. Get off right now." If I was him, I would'a been scared. She sounded cuttin mean.

He smiled. "Ma'am, you know I'm a federal agent. You know why I'm here." His head jerked when he heard me ready Pops' rifle. "No need for any trouble, here. Y'all just go back home and let me take care of business, then I'll go away. No one gets hurt."

I gulped when Mama stood and aimed her rifle. I shook when I stood beside her, aimin, for the first time ever, right at a real live person. When I remember that day, this part comes to me in slow motion. I think it's like that for terrible events. And this was one.

He whipped his revolver and dropped the ax in the same second. Mama was ready to fire her rifle, but didn't. She saw what I saw. I was lookin down the barrel of a killin weapon 'bout 15 feet away. The weapon aimed at my chest, and it looked like a bullseye.

"So, now, this seems like a good time to do the smart thing and throw those rifles out here." He smiled evil. He was sure of himself now. He felt in cocky-control.

"Don't hurt my boy. We'll do what you say, mister. Just take it easy. Eugene, I want you to relax your grip on that rifle. Good. Now I want you to pitch it out there like the man says. Do it easy so's not to damage your Pops' rifle. Okay, son?" Mama talked very slow and soft.

"Yes, Mama." I saw that Mama never took her eyes off the agent and his weapon, even as she talked to me, but that he looked back and forth, from me to Mama. I'd seen Mama hunt all kind of critters in the woods. She was fast, and had a sharp eye. I wonder about the cocky agent?

I slowly made a show of getting the rifle in the right position to pitch it out, away from our protective wall. Then I thought to actually pitch it as far as I could, givin some distraction to the situation. And he did it. The agent looked at the rifle as it arced in the air. And Mama's rifle fired, droppin that man dead in the dirt.

The echo of the shot was all around us, bouncin off'a trees, and in my ears. I felt sick but stood there, beside my Mama. We both stared at the lifeless agent, who would'a shot me dead if it came to that. She was still holdin tight to that rifle.

"Want me to take that, Mama?"

She turned to me, dropped the rifle, and wrapped her arms around me. I could feel her shiver, but when she talked, she sounded strong.

"I'm sorry that had to happen, son. Weren't nothin you should have 'ta see. You are strong, like your father. He'll be proud of you."

She was quiet for a bit, then remembered. "I'm just glad Annie didn't have to see this."

No, Annie wasn't home when this day turned wrong. She was at the church, havin kid's Bible class. I remembered what the Pastor said earlier that very day, but did the Lord really make this day?

Mama stayed with the dead agent while I ran back to the house to wait for Pops. And if he didn't show in a bit, I was to head out to find him. I waited long as I could stand, then started runnin fast as I could. 'Bout a mile down the road, Pops' truck screeched to a halt to pick me up. He knew somethin was wrong. I filled him in as we headed back.

Pops assessed the situation as safe, then hugged Mama. We hadn't touched the body, and there was a muddy red pool soakin into the ground around it. Pops and me went into the trees and brush until we came out on the road and found the dead man's gray car.

"Your Mama will have a hard time with this. We ain't never gonna talk about it, again, even now. Just do what I tell ya, then we'll go home."

Mama had already gone home to be there for Annie. I was wishin I could'a gone, too. But, I had a responsibility to my folks and I wasn't about to show how scared I was.

Pops pulled an old tarp from the shed near the still, and we rolled up the agent. Never got the man's name. Guess it don't matter, anyway. As hard as I tried not to look, I saw his face, the worst thing I would ever lay my eyes on in my whole life. I turned away and Pops slowed down a bit to let me throw up tomato and some of my breakfast, then we commenced to pullin the guy down the hill to his sedan. His last ride in that fancy car.

We both stood by the side of the road, listenin for any oncomin traffic. I opened the trunk and we pitched him in. Dad took the wheel and started the car. Smooth engine just purred. There was no one around at Bo's place. Bo done been laid to rest in the town cemetery, a real nice burial. Most everbody came for the send-off. In a few days, the menfolk would be up here pushin Bo's burnt-up house into one of the deepest ravines in Bell County. Heard tell it was miles deep. I stayed far back from that edge.

"Look at his shoes, boy, nothing else," Pops warned me. Guess he didn't want me to barf again. Me neither. We unloaded him from the trunk and unrolled him into the front seat. Pops said he would need that tarp for other uses, no need to throw it into the ravine. I don't remember what the guy's shoes looked like.

"Now, listen to exactly what I tell ya. I don't want ya goin over the edge with that city slicker's car. Mo-mentum can do that to ya. When I yell drop, you drop flat on the ground, lettin go of the car. Understand?"

"Yes, sir, I do." My eyes felt like they was buggin out of my head. I hadn't thought about mo-mentum. I knew he could see me shakin real bad. But, I wanted to make him proud more'n anything. I did what Pops said.

The outside of the car was gettin a little warm, settin in the hot sun. We laid hands on the tail-end and pushed with all our might. Shortly, it started takin on speed. I was so danged scared I was cryin.

"Drop, drop, drop!" screamed Pops.

I fell flat on my belly, but Pops pushed a bit longer. I thought he was a goner, then he dropped, just at the edge of that ravine. At first, the car made a heck of a lot of noise, hittin trees and rocks. After a bit, it got harder to hear, like the trees were whisperin, as it kept goin. Then it was quiet.

I wiped my wet eyes, but stayed right where I was. Ain't never been this tired or scared in my life. Didn't move until Pops slowly got up, first on his hands and knees, then to his feet. I grabbed his offered hand and stood in front of him. He nodded at me, and I felt his pride.

I followed him to a fallen log, where we sat. He pulled out his pack of chew and offered me some.

"Thank you, sir, but do ya happen to have your pipe on ya?"

He laughed and pulled the pipe from an inside pocket of the vest he was wearin. I felt him watchin as I proceeded to light it for the first time.

"Too bad," I said, "it was a nice car."

"Hmph. Just a city-slicker car. Ya got anything ya need to talk about, young man? Last chance."

"No sir, I don't think I do." And I took my first draw from my daddy's pipe, just like I always watched him do.

The Bouncer

As Steve surveyed the balls remaining on the pool table he knew that he would be 10 bucks to the good in just a short time. He straightened his body, all 6–foot–three of him, thoroughly enjoying the tension produced by the delay. Mad Mike was a friend, but Steve never minded taking money from a friend in a fair game.

Mad Mike wasn't cool or patient like his friend, he didn't like delays or tension. "What the hell you waiting on, boy, chest hair?"

Steve grinned, just to irritate Mike a little. He stretched his arms above his head, flexing his muscles and his lean body.

Steve and Mike were close; they would bleed for each other, already had, more than once. Mike wouldn't seriously get mad at Steve; but, he could get mad, damned mad. Got his nickname by proving it. Not many people messed with Mike; no one messed with him twice. The same for Steve.

Mike was tall, half a head taller than Steve, had ragged brown hair down to his shoulders; his bearded face was scarred and pocked. He tucked his black jeans into black leather boots with chains dangling from the sides and spurs on the heels that spun and clinked with warning as he walked. Some called called ugly, but not to his face. He addressed women he met as sweetheart and hon, as long as they didn't prove otherwise.

Steve tipped the wet brown bottle to his smiling lips, slowly, tauntingly...enjoying the biting coolness as the liquid slid down his throat.

The pale flesh around Steve's large blue eyes remained crinkled and his eyebrows raised as he emptied the bottle, the whole time seemingly ignoring mad Mike's annoyance. He ran his long fingers through his wheat colored hair; he rubbed his chin, deep in thought.

"Well, this is a tough one, Mike; but I think I figured it out," quipped Steve, always on top of his game. Steve tried not to show that he was a little off his game, tired from an extra late night playing poker. Being distracted in these rooms can get a body hurt. Even when playing pool or poker with a friend, flinching can be unforgiving.

"If you have to take this much time, boy, you might just need to get yourself a job at Kmart," joked Mike, followed by a growling chuckle.

Just as Steve was positioning himself, his lean, muscled body becoming one with the green felt, visualizing the balls sinking, one after another, into their worn, velvet pockets, a bottle shattered against the wall behind him, spraying beer and glass halfway down the wall and onto the floor. He whirled, wide-eyed, taut and primed, his left hand quickly reaching back to make sure the 38 snub-nose was in place and as ready as he was.

The bottle came from about 15 feet away. A small crowd was gathering at that end of the bar. Years of patronizing and working these sleazy joints had taught Steve to ignore other people's minor arguments, and to cautiously tune in to escalating ones. This one had erupted with a vengeance, fast and ugly.

"You stupid bitch. I oughta kill you."

Steve's powerful muscled arms were around the man he knew only as Frank within seconds of the exploding beer bottle. He knew him slightly, knew that he drank too much, had a quick temper, and that his name was Frank. He had never fought him or played cards with him.

"Get your fucking hands off me!" Frank yelled as he struggled to pull free from Steve's fixed grip.

This is not the way Steve had planned to spend the afternoon. He had been playing poker late into the night and early morning hours, drank too much, slept too little. He was trying to ease into the day, giving his head time to quit exploding.

As Steve drug Frank away from the woman, he looked her way. He knew her; he had tried to ignore her when she first wobbled in a couple hours ago. She had been quiet till now, not grating his last nerve like she could, and had, in the past. She was a stupid bitch. She looked like hell today. She was holding herself precariously against the bar with the aid of locked elbows; her head wobbled as she tried to maintain focus on her attacker.

She was skinny; would have passed for dead if she wasn't standing. Steve couldn't figure out why anyone would want to get into a fight over her, much less screw her. Nevertheless, he had done both, himself, not so long ago. Somehow, she knew how to turn the screws on a guy until his nerves were raw, then turn on the charm and make everything seem better for a while. The woman was nuts and made people around her nuts, too. She had tormented Steve in the past, but not long ago enough for him.

"That's right", she slurred, trying hard to appear indignant, "drag his ass out of here. Who does he think he is, calling me a bitch? He's just a rag to wipe...."

"You shut up!" Steve yelled her way. Frank was not taking his ouster well, and Steve was in no mood to listen to Lou's crap, too. Frank was not as tall as Steve, but he was strong. They both lifted weights in the back room of the same bar along the Seventh Street strip. Frank cursed Steve, Lou, the bar, and a few people that Steve had never heard of. The whole time he continually struggled to wrestle himself free, jabbing without much success.

"Dammit, Frank. Just calm yourself down and I'll let you go. You keep this shit up, and I'll have to knock the hell out of you." He felt sorry for the poor bastard for getting mixed up with Lou and didn't particularly want to fight him.

"You think you're big shit, don't you!" Frank spat over his shoulder. "Come up behind a guy like that. Face me up punk. I'll show you what big is."

"Damn you!" Frank had slung spittle across Steve's right hand and had found the end of his captor's patience. Steve had merely been doing his job. Now he was pissed off.

The small crowd in the bar recognized the change and began to move farther away. Up till now the duo had provided splendid entertainment, but no one knew what might happen next. Mad Mike, who'd been lounging across the pool table, sat up for a better view, cocking his head slightly, wrinkling his brow. Mad Mike knew that Steve had been in many bar fights, most of the time came out the winner; somebody was about to get hurt. Mad Mike liked to see a good fight, and didn't mind the sight of blood.

Steve deftly twisted Frank's right arm so that he groaned and bent over in pain, falling to his knees. Steve's powerful knee crushed against Frank's back sending him facedown onto the sticky black floor. Blood oozed from Frank's nose, along his left upper lip, and into the curve of his mouth. One hand was free, one was pinned under his chest, and he was pinned under Steve's unrelenting knee.

Lou's legs finally gave out, and her grip on the bar loosened under the weight; she slid from the bar to the floor. The door to the men's restroom opened and a regular known as Doc weaved his way over to the bar and slid down beside Lou.

"What you doing down here, sweetheart?"

She pointed an unsteady finger toward Steve and Frank, leaned against Doc, and whispered, "Those two got in a fight. We're watching."

Steve yelled toward the bar, "Get me a wet towel for chrissake!" He held his prisoner with little effort while he washed the spit from his arm, a grimace of disgust shadowing his face. "Listen, Frank. I think we've had enough of this stupid game. Don't you?"

"You broke my damn nose! Why'd you break my damn nose, Steve?"

"I'm going to let you up, Frank," Steve growled. "Then I want your ass out that door fast, or I'll kick it out. And you find another place to pull your shit; you come back here and I'll break your nose again, just for the hell of it."

Steve released his grip, stepped back, and waited, noticing a dark, wet, blue denim stain spreading around Frank's crotch. He wouldn't be any more trouble, Steve thought. Steve had a way of reading people fairly well; he was still breathing after many such encounters.

Frank pulled himself up slowly, one knee at a time moving up under his belly. His body drooped there, on all fours; the blood dripped slowly from his nose creating a peculiar design on the worn linoleum. He watched it for a slow-motion kind of eternity, then, finally, pulled himself up and started walking toward the door. He paused when he saw a grinning Mad Mike holding the door wide open. As soon as he passed through, Mad Mike bowed at the waist with an arm sweep, then, let the door slam just short of smacking Frank's aching ass.

Mike leaned over, hands on his knees, guffawing from somewhere deep inside. When he straightened, he had to swipe tears from his eyes with the top of his T-shirt. "Hell, Steve, that stupid piece of crap ain't never seen you mad, now has he?"

The tension in the air was already easing, drinkers were turning back to the bar, a deck of cards being shuffled whispered from a dark corner, someone whistled softly.

"Yeah. Well, he never spit on me before, either," Steve yelled from the sink. Mike headed for the toilet, laughing and shaking his head, spurs chinking the whole way.

Steve turned and stared down at the two bodies stretched out at the foot of the bar. "Doc. You get her out of here now! I don't ever want to see her scrawny face in here again."

He looked at Lou, instigator, manipulator. Steve slowly squatted down, face-to-face with one of the women of his nightmares. His voice was cold, sure, piercing. "You hear me, Lou, don't come back. Go anywhere but here. Go to hell if you want. Just get out."

"Aw, come on," Doc protested in ignorance. "Why you get mad at her. She ain't saying nothing."

Steve heard the door crash against the wall and felt the vibration through the floor at the same time. He stood and swung around in time to see the gleaming eight inch blade penetrate his gut. He watched as the last four inches passed into his body. The flesh separated like warm butter. The slight resistance of toned muscle fought this unwanted advance. A cold shudder coursed through him as the point reamed through his belly; the almost soothing warmth of his own blood ran freely. Before his legs buckled under him, his left arm tensed, his hand clinched, and his fist crashed into Frank's nose. Silence.

Frank heard the chink of the chains and spurs as the large boots hit heavy on the floor behind him. Barstools rattled as customers ducked in fear. Someone threw up. He left the knife in Steve's gut and began the turn toward the door, but Mike had him before he took his first step, His massive hands folded around Frank's neck, and Frank's body sailed across the room, "like a damn paper airplane," according to Doc, and hit the wall. Posters on their flea market frames jumped right off their nails, at least two landing on Frank's head, cutting his right ear lobe, "clear in half, by gawd," according to Doc, again.

Warm bodies spilled onto the sidewalk, following the call of the sirens and lights. They came from the neighboring adult toy store one door away, from the tattoo shop, and from the White Castle across the street. They came to see whatever there was to see, and to listen to Doc. His red face beamed as he told his story to the hungry crowd. "Like a damn paper airplane," he repeated. "Reached out and punched him smack in his broken nose. Pow!" he fed his followers.

The crowd parted in silence, craning their necks as the men in blue carried the stretcher to the waiting ambulance. "That's not him," Doc spoke with authority. The crowd surged together again. Waiting. Trying to see inside.

"If I die, kill that bitch. Promise me, Mike." Steve clasped Mike's hand with a strength that equaled that which had already been sucked from his body. "And, don't tell my mother; not ...this, she can't..."

"You got it, man. I love ya. You got it". Mike didn't see the paramedics who carried the stretcher. He only saw Steve disappearing behind the double doors, and a snake coiling around the sword. And he saw that through a wet haze of tears.

The Pendulum Swings

I fumble with the keys and almost drop them. It's silly to feel this nervous; nothing unusual will happen tonight. My hands feel numb, and I tremble, pitiful, like the sickly tree in the side yard when a storm comes along. Old Doctor Sanders says I'm fine and healthy, and that when my body adjusts to my newfound pastime of walking the troubling feelings would stop. That's been months; of course, I didn't tell him everything, now did I?

Walking is good for me; I have probably never been in such good shape physically. I have more energy than ever before, but, sometimes, I am so very tired. I snap the deadbolt. The lemon scent of hot wax from the candle I had snuffed out before I left the house for my walk is still in the air.

After all these years, my whole life, I still listen as the weight of my body presses down on the creaky floorboards that lead to the kitchen. As long as I can remember, those same boards have sounded alarms, and told secrets.

When we were kids, Jerry and I would sneak down the steps at night, knowing which steps to pass over, which boards in the hall would give us away, as we would steal into the kitchen for the tiniest sliver of cake from Sunday dinner. If we took a terribly tiny piece mother might not notice; there'd be hell to pay if she did. It was the adventure, the daring, the mystery of moving in the darkness, with hearts pounding, that was sweeter than any pie or cake found in our kitchen.

Mother was very stingy, withholding in every way. She prepared some kind of dessert on Saturday nights for Sunday dinner; one small piece for everyone, meticulously sliced by her. A little extra would have been nice now and then. No harm in a little kindness from that woman. Never.

Shadows and pale light peep into the kitchen through the shutters at the little window over the sink. Reaching for the light switch, I feel like that little girl again, and hesitate, the memory so close, so real. The switch clicks and the kitchen is bathed in the fluorescent light. My kitchen, now. Mother would never have these lights in her house because she thought there was something evil about a light that didn't just blink on or off. Fluorescent lights are in the bathroom, too. My bathroom. I'll make more changes as time goes by.

The dishes I used earlier, still soak in the sink; I smell the strong lemony detergent. I hate the smell of lemon; it's been in this house for so long. What, a sound? No, just the clock ticking. Guess I'll clean the dishes My thoughts are on soothing, hot water, a long soak in a hot bath, and settling down to read or maybe just think.

Quietly up the stairs making sure that I avoid the squeaky steps. The grimace that is forcing its way on my lips tells me that the memories will be strong tonight. On nights like this memories surround, sometimes smother me like a heavy wool blanket. Lord, doesn't a wool blanket smell awful when it is wet, especially if it is green. I don't know why that is but rough, green wool blankets smell worse than anything else, especially when they're wet.

I had that one green wool blanket on my bed when I was such a little girl. I wet the bed and mother found out, heard me moving around in my room; she made me wrap up in that wet, wool blanket and sleep on the floor for the rest of the night, cold and shivering. I think I was six years old, then. She screamed at me. She was so mad. She said every horrible thing to me that could be said to a six year old girl in stinking, wet pajamas. She wouldn't let me take a bath before I went to school the next morning. I washed off as best I could with toilet paper. Lord, if I used a washcloth she would have known that I had not obeyed her. That blanket was found burned nearly to ashes in the back yard the next day. Poor Jerry got the spunk knocked right out of him by dad. "I miss you, Jerry."

Softly close the bathroom door. Turn on the steamy hot water.

Tonight I will splurge and use bath oil. I can't use oil every night. It wouldn't be so special anymore; and I need some things to be special now and then.

My clothes slide into a soft pile and I feel soft for a moment, relaxed. Naked body sliding into the bubbling water.

It nearly takes my breath away! My whole body is stinging. It's, well, it's sensuous, so wonderful. It sounds like a word that conjures up images of sex, but sex was never so wonderful. I tried it a few times, long ago. There I go, ruining what is supposed to be a relaxing bath. My time. I'm going to concentrate on these bubbles; nothing more. That is what I need right now, to think about nothing. My brain is exhausted with all the thinking, the memories, fantasies, the planning.

I had a school project, a paper to write, about a time when I was scared or confused. At ten years old, there were already many possibilities. But there was one that made me physically sick when I thought of it. I never knew if it was a nightmare or a real event.

"Mother." She stood at the sink with her hands in soapy water. "Did I ever almost drown?" I waited quietly, swallowed and trembled when she stood still and quiet.

She stopped moving her hands in the dishwater. "What are you babbling about now?"

"I think I had a dream, but it seems so real. So I was wondering if it was. There was water between you and me, and you were smiling, I think. So, it should be a good dream, but I was scared, real scared."

She turned and stared straight into my eyes. That always scared the crap out of me. "Tell me more about this ridiculous dream of yours."

"I think I saw Daddy behind you. And I heard yelling and banging, like on a door. I'm not real sure. When I dream about it now, I wake up choking."

She threw her head back and laughed. "You'd better write about something that makes sense, girl. I want to read that story before you turn it in. Don't want your teacher thinking you're a dimwit."

Nothing puts me on edge like a dissatisfying bath. I should be relaxed, but I'm tense, shaky. It's not just the bath, of course; it's this feeling that has been growing for over a month, longer. It began when I bought the shoes. I remember telling myself that I would never really do it, that it was completely out of the question. But, I knew I would have to, sooner or later. No real choice in the matter.

~.~

After staring in ignorance, through the storefront window, at all the different kinds of shoes that could possibly be labeled sneakers, I sucked in my breath and swallowed all the air I could and went in. The store had been practically empty; it was a Wednesday. That young man, probably in his mid-twenties, offered to help me in any way that I needed. Sure. "I want some shoes that would be good for walking briskly," I had told him. He seemed to think that he knew exactly what I needed. I paid him $34.95, and started for home. I felt numb. I dropped the new shoes in a bag with *other purchases of the day: a book by some famous doctor from California*

who believes that walking is the key to the fountain of youth, and a set of

royal blue sweats for my new past-time. I would hate to go unnoticed.

When I got home I threw the bag into the closet in my bedroom,

shaking my head in disbelief for making such a foolish purchase. That bag

lay untouched for two weeks before I was able to reach in for the book. I

read it from cover to cover before I started walking; everything had to be

done just right.

~.~

I pad quietly to my room; the towel draped around my hot, damp

body feels cozy. It is an ordinary night. I am doing ordinary things. But am

I? Feeling drawn to look into the mirror, I see the reflection of a woman

who is often a stranger to me. Dropping the towel, staring, a disinterested

party. How can this mirror, the same one that once reflected a wide-eyed

little girl in pigtails, now reflect a soft, not quite flabby, middle aged

woman? I've lost weight in the past month, I guess from the walking; or

from feeling nauseous from the smell of lemon. I think I was pretty as a

child, but certainly not as a woman. I see creases between my brows, and

tight lines around the corners of the mouth. I'm never happy to see the resemblance of mother and daughter. I practice sneering at myself in the mirror. She sneers back. Bitch.

~.~

Long ago I stood in front of this mirror and watched myself cry until my face was puffy and my head pounded with pain. I almost cried once after that, but didn't. That night had started as a date with the most popular boy in school; the kind of boy most girls dream about, but never realize the dream coming true. I was only allowed to go to school functions, and should never refer to anything as a date. This did not make me a popular girl, as if I would have been anyway. He was a senior and I knew he was going through as many girls as possible before he decided who he was going to take to the prom. I did everything to attract his attention except take out an ad in the school paper. Yes, I even let him cop a few feels by my locker. I was thrilled and terrified when he asked me out, but it seemed like it was a chance for something wonderful to happen in my life.

Mother surprised us on the back porch, and if his ring had not snagged on my sweater, we might have been able to regain some semblance of decency before she turned on the yellow porch light. She was a maniac. I had never seen anything like it before. He ran. Mother

screamed for Dad to chase after him and to tell his parents. Jerry tried to

calm her down but she was hysterical until she swung her arm back and

slapped me so hard that I fell backwards into a table that kept me from

falling to the floor. In a gurgling growl she ordered me to my room. That

was the last night I cried. I hurt on so many levels. I couldn't bear facing

kids at school, could barely make it through the front doors , forgot my

locker number on a weekly basis and started skipping lunch. I have been

walking in a blur most of my life, trying to not be seen.

That was the last night I cried for any reason. That was the year dad

died; I suspect his heart just couldn't take anymore. Three months later

Jerry left me alone with her. He tied a rope around his neck and kicked his

desk chair. His chess set pieces were strewn all about the room; she

crawled around picking up all those little game pieces while the sheriff cut

her son down and lay him on his bed for the last time. I was totally alone.

~.~

My gown is so soft and feels gentle next to so many harsh memories.

There were some good; there had to be; I just can't think of any now. I

pad down the stairs in soft house shoes to fix hot-cocoa. I look forward to steamy hot cocoa and date nut bread. Just the thought makes me feel better. Hmm, the thought – most of my feelings are based on a thought, usually a memory; no wonder then that I am usually in a bad mood. Maybe this evening won't be so bad after all. I take my goodies back to my room. Avoid the noisy steps. Stop to listen. Nothing. But the ticking of the clock, and later the chimes.

The cocoa is good. The music soothing, classical, soft. So warm and comfortable. I could stay like this forever. I gaze lazily around the room, in tune with the music. The good feelings slide away like the towel had earlier. The shoes are staring at me from the corner.

Again they remind me of their purpose, my plan, the pattern I have developed. No one would know how well it was all thought out. It was really just a simple diversion, though. I would never be able to do it. It is just not the sort of thing ordinary people do. And no one is more ordinary than I.

Well, fine and dandy. All the warm, comfortable feelings and sensations are gone. Isn't that the way it always happens. There will never be peace in my life as long as....I suppose I should check. Isn't that what I'm here for? My total existence for one purpose only, every day a drudge. Bitch.

Day after day, week after week, somehow became year after year. Dreams forgotten; life ignored. So much time gone by almost unnoticed. How can that be? How can whole years pass without something significant to mark them; without something wonderful, spectacular, or even tragic occurring to jar one's sense of existence?

Holidays or birthdays mean nothing when living is emptiness; they were important to a little girl once. Occasions don't really exist when there is no one to share them with. People alone, people like me, enjoy a warm bath and a cup of hot chocolate much more than Christmas.

I hate breakfast, a necessary ritual. But, now that I have the mess cleaned up in the kitchen, I'll spend a few quiet moments on the back porch with the newspaper. God! Before I know it, it will be lunch time. Again! I need time to myself, days to myself. I want my life to start. The morning has been particularly trying. A deep breath. This is my time.

"I don't believe it. I don't," I said out loud, as I read the article about an old friend. Should I hate her? She was my friend once upon a time. She seemed so dense to me then; always wanted to study with me. Now she has her face plastered on the local newspaper again. She is on her third husband. "Third!" all of them rich; and I, I have no one. Why is she so free to do whatever she wants, while I just exist.

Is my life as bleak as I imagine? Perhaps if I did something different, something new. "That's really funny, missy," mumbling to myself. I, by God, am doing something different. As for new, the walking shoes are new, and my walking clothes. Ah, the new me.

But I don't feel new. I don't really feel any better. Today is one of the worst days of my life. I wake up in a sweat from a frightening dream, then breakfast – extremely trying. Then the article about that slut marrying yet another wealthy man. Lunch no better-even worse. I think I hate her. I hate most everybody. There certainly is no one on this earth that I love; Jerry saw to that. I hate life; I hate myself. "Why not!"

Oh, my head, the throbbing. Nothing seems to help but to bury my head in the darkness of a soft pillow. It's her fault. All of it. The throbbing, the palpitations, the anger, the guilt. The loneliness. Isolation. These are my life; a death sentence.

So this is it. There is no more time to think or plan. That was all done long ago, probably even before I was even consciously aware of it. I'll do it. I must do it. For the first time I'll really take charge, make a decision and execute it; for once.

The park is just busy enough, as I had hoped it would be. There are enough people here so that I will surely be able to pass by and speak to several that I know from the neighborhood. But, not so many that I will simply be another face in the crowd.

I did not think that I would feel this way. Lord, I feel weak and shaky, even nauseous. Still, I am invigorated; I do feel that; I know I do. I finally made an important life decision for myself and I will carry it out. My only regret is that I can't tell everyone how clever I am. They will never know. I won't end up in the newspaper like Sally slut, smiling triumphantly. Some things we just don't need to know.

Neither will I be able to gather the sympathy I want by telling people what a hell I've been living all these years. The only person who would understand is Jerry, and he deserted me long ago.

There's Mrs. Martin. I wave. She smiles at me. Good. All is right in the world.

I'll never be able to tell anyone how I hate my own mother. Every day the hate grows larger and larger until I'm painfully consumed with her.

She did that to me. Still does. All the years of depending on her icy hand for my physical needs, and looking to her stony heart, searching for comfort. Before I had the courage to leave or make the same decision as Jerry, she turned the tables on me and she hated me for it.

For years now I have taken care of her physical needs, while she lay helpless in her bed. That is all she requires from me. But the cruel, despising glare that follows my every move sucks my strength. I feel her slotted eyes on my back when I turn away, and often I want to just run away in fear, run and cry. More than once I'll catch her reflection in the dresser mirror as I precisely fold and put away her clothes; sneering, cruel, dark and ugly. Her look makes me shiver. I hate her and fear her.

Today is different. I will never fear her again, but, alas, I will always hate her.

As I walk back toward home I make a point of speaking to a few people in close proximity to my house. Yes, I smile and speak. I'm in control, finally.

I close the door after I enter the house, and walk up the steps. I check on my dear invalid mother. I look around one last time to make certain that everything is in order. Of course there is nothing out of order, but I check anyway. Being precise was always important to mother. She'll appreciate that.

There, the nice fluffy pillow is tucked under her head just so, as it should be, always was.

"Help! Help!," I scream as I run down the steps to call the sheriff. "Hurry," I say, "I think she is dead!" Please hurry, yeah, take your damn time. The witch is dead. I smothered the hateful hag with her own precious pillow so that I can live, finally live. When the clock strikes twelve tonight, and the chimes chime, not only a new day will be rung in, but a new life. Mine! All mine.

~.~

I sit alone. The empty faces, the condolences, all gone. Nothing unexpected. All the usual town mourners came to the party, ate the food, droned on about painless endings. And now it's over. The house is quiet. At last. I didn't like those people in my house. Just because someone dies, they think they are entitled to three-day squatters rights, put on dark clothes, a face and move in until the food is gone. But it's over now. I can finally live a life that will be all about me.

What I need is a steamy bath, and a cup of hot cocoa by the light of a candle, perhaps. It has been a long day – a long year. I can barely keep my eyes open. The room is warm, bathed in the glow from the single flame.

Downstairs, the clock is ticking, pendulum swinging to time – nearly midnight.

That strange dream I had, as if I were yet to be born, perhaps another chance at life. **I am sensing on at least two levels (as dreams can go)...I am in an upstairs room (very large finished attic or bonus room)...it is very bright and spacious...Everything is pink...I am pondering over "them", the people downstairs, wanting me to stay with them. They want this very much...but I look around the room and it is very sparse, not like I am staying for long...I look for clothes to put on and realize I did not come prepared so I must not be staying long or not at all...still, I look for a suitcase...the sparse furniture blends in with the pink walls, barren comes to mind.**

I am at the table with them...but not. I sense that there are two children there, but the parents want me to stay, although I never see their faces. I see how they will provide for me, wanting to make everything special. I see my place at the table.

I am back in the pink room. I feel bad for them because I am still not sure. I look down the long, steep staircase...pink. It looks daunting...I just don't think I will be here long...

At precisely 10:00, I open the front door, shaking off the heaviness of the night and the dream, and step out into a fresh new day. I take a deep breath, stretch my arms, glance at my shoes, and start my easy run, having graduated just recently from walking, which grew tedious. Several blocks down Maple, crossing over to Elm, I wave to the Mayor's wife having tea on her beautiful side porch with her dog, Poopsie, in her lap, and on toward the park. I enjoy the fresh, slightly warm air on my face, and for the first time I feel freedom. It is, indeed, my time to be alive.

But shouldn't I have known, surely I should have learned, that life can't be simple or predictable. I couldn't have known that shortly after I wave to the Mayor's wife, Mrs. Bellow, she would have a stroke and never be able to wave or to pet Poopsie again. I couldn't have known that the couple living next door to me were talking about divorce over eggs and toast at that very moment. Or that my favorite elementary school teacher just became a grandmother. And I certainly could not have known that across town a foolish young man would run from the town bank with a gun in one hand and a bag in the other, while his girlfriend waits in his junky van for a quick getaway, and that their timing was off.

It would not have made much difference to know all these things. I look ahead at the park growing closer with each pat of my feet on the ground. I hear the shrill laughter of school children on an outing, and am distracted enough that it's really too late when I finally hear the brakes squealing around the corner and all I feel in that last moment is the powerful impact of the grill of a rusty van .

Celebration of Life:
A Mother's Challenge

I've known it for many years, since he was an older teenager. He didn't come out until he settled in San Francisco, far from home, apparently where gay men go to get away from unaccepting family. He was a good boy and turned into a good man, in spite of his parents.

My husband is his stepdad...I don't know if that made a difference or not in the way they despise each other. But I'm sitting here waiting for my flight call to board thinking these thoughts because I don't know what else to do with myself.

"Would you feel better if I was going with you?" my husband, Phil, asked.

"Shane doesn't want you there. It's a mute subject."

"Don't have to be grouchy with me. I didn't cause this."

"Really? Are you purposely trying to start an argument, or are you just feeling guilty?" I turn away from him just a little. I sigh loud enough for him to hear.

"Now just a minute, there. I don't have a thing to feel guilty about. I know this is hard on you. But, dammit it all, I didn't have anything to do with Shane being gay, and that's what this is all about."

I hate flying and I hate airports. Right now, I'm also irritable to the inth degree with my husband. I'd like to hit him over the head with my overstuffed purse, but that's not something we've ever done...laid a hand on each other. He had the boys for that.

"That's my call to board," I say as he kisses my cheek.

"I'm sorry, Irene. Call me when you can."

I find my seat and start rifling through my purse, just for something to do. I eat some mints I find at the bottom. There's no way to stop thinking about what lies ahead.

I'm going to San Francisco to be with my son when he dies. He has scheduled his death, the time, place and participants. It's like a ghastly dream, not something I can talk to anyone about and ask for the proper protocol..."So, what did you wear to your son's death?" and crap like that. Please don't let anyone ask me where I'm going. I'll stare straight out the window the whole time. Got ear buds to send a visual message, "Leave me the hell alone."

I'm angry at myself and my husband for not being better parents. I'm so damned mad at Phil for being such a badass, and myself for not standing up for my boys more. What else could I have expected when he was retired military and now working as a guard at the state prison. I never expected him to be soft-hearted. Wish we had girls instead. He's good with the girls in the family.

This isn't his fault. What am I doing? I hurt so badly I want to be mad at anyone but my son. But I am. It is his fault, dammit! But he didn't know. He got the disease. He didn't plan to. And it will kill him.

He is a kind, gentle soul. Everyone loves Shane. His huge, toothy grin makes everyone around him smile...except for his step-dad. From the time he was a toddler he developed an endearing sense of humor, and along with his smile, invited everyone into his circle.

What am I going to do when I get there? I just don't know how I can do whatever I'm expected to do. Shane and his partner have made all the plans. I feel so alone, useless. My son didn't even want either of his brothers to be there.

I feel shudders through my body when I hear, "Would you like something to drink?" I can't look up. What now. "Excuse me, ma'am, but would you like a drink or snack?"

"Sprite, no ice." I can see the ice when my shaky hands send it flying across the cabin, scaring the shit out of somebody. By the time I drink this, we will be almost to Chicago where I change planes. I'll probably miss my flight. I shouldn't have come alone, no matter what he said. I'm not too sound of mind right now. So, I'll spend the rest of the day staring out this damn window.

~.~

There's my name spelled out in capital letters on a white board. So, that's Paul. He's nice looking. He's smiling like it hurts when our eyes meet. "Irene?" he asks.

"Paul," is all I can say. I let tears gush all over him and he wraps his arms around me. I can't let him know what I'm thinking. I feel horrible for wishing it was him and not my Shane. Why my son for God's sake? I would still have come to support my son as his partner died if it was the other way around. But Paul was clean...no HIV, no Aides.

They must truly care deeply for each other, and for that I'm grateful. Shane was never alone from the time he was diagnosed. But soon, my boy will be dead and his partner will go on. Somehow, I will, too. Not a damn thing in life is fair.

Paul drives smoothly through the hellish traffic, pointing out a few of Shane's favorite places, as if he is trying to introduce me to the man he knows and loves. A different person that I don't really know. It was an unspoken rule that Shane was always welcome, but to never bring that other part of his life into our home. We couldn't deal with it. No. That's not it...my husband wouldn't deal with it.

"Paul, what do I do when we get there? How can I help? Well, except, of course for the...you know." I hope he doesn't think me disgusting for sniffing as tears roll down my face. I look ahead, not seeing much of anything. I'm not focusing well.

"Everything is planned, but try to be normal, I guess. If you can. There will be a sort of party, like a wake. At least Shay will get to enjoy it."

I flinch when I hear him refer to my son by a name I've never heard, but try not to be too obvious. There are a lot of things I don't know about his life. I only know the son that visits and swims and plays cards late into the night. If his brothers are there, they drink beer and cackle over Saturday Night Live. That always made me laugh, even though I don't like the show itself.

"He wants to make sure you have some time alone with him, if you want. Sunday night is when it will happen. He hasn't decided the time, yet, but that's no big deal."

I can't help myself. I want to claw his eyes out. "How can you say it's 'no big deal'?"

"I'm sorry, Irene. I meant that Shay said he would decide later, when it felt right." His face tightened in pain as he stared ahead and drove the car. A yellow Volkswagen, convertible. Clean inside. It must be hell for him to put up with Shane, such a slob. He used to be. I don't really know my son anymore. How can I live without him on this earth? Too much to demand of a mother. I won't bother to wipe the tears. They aren't going to stop until I'm dry.

I could be looking out the window, get a good look at the city. I'd already visited Shane a few times, but we met without his partner. He took me to all the main tourist spots, took me to his work where he introduced to me his co-workers. It fit him. Laid back. He seemed so at home in his health food store. Everyone admired him. They had no choice...that's the kind of guy he is. My baby.

~.~

"There's an elevator in the back if you're not okay with the steps. Just one floor up."

"I'm good with the steps." He started the climb carrying all my stuff. "Paul." He stopped and looked around, with a furrowed brow. "I need you to know how much I appreciate that you have stayed with Shane through this. I know it can't be easy." He came back to stand in front of me and dropped the bags.

His arms encircle me. Until this moment I didn't know how badly I need a hug, some human affection. We do share something very important. I'm startled slightly when he says, "We share something big, Irene. We both love him enough to be here, no matter how hard it is."

I'm counting the steps, and the climb is eternity. We stop at the door and stare. This is a freakin dream, the kind that never ends, just moves from one hell-hole to the next. And Paul opens the door. I see Shane's smile as soon as I step into their apartment. He is curled up on his left side in a hospital-bed, which takes a lot of the living room space.

Paul takes my bags away while I hold my son in my arms. We both cry like babies until we run out of energy. "I love the beard, Shane. I don't remember you ever growing one." It's soft. I run my hands down the length of it. We look into each other's eyes, searching for the connection.

He laughed softly and ran his left hand over the mess of hair on his chin. "I want to go out mucho macho." His voice more a whisper. All I see are bones and veins. His hand so thin, and translucent, in spite of bruised flesh. "I'm so glad you're here, Mom. I wish I'd been a better son, one you could be proud of."

"Alright. Now I'm setting some rules here. None of this apologizing stuff. I wish I'd been a better mother, too. But we have just a bit of time here to just love each other. If there is anything you need to say, to rant and rave, do it. But I don't need any sorrys from you. I've loved you forever and will when you're...gone"

Shane managed another smile, not the big smile that was contagious, a weak but meaningful one. "I lovya, Mom." He is already sounding exhausted.

I put my index finger on his lips gently and say, "Shush. I love you, too."

Paul came in with water for Shane. He sipped, slightly choked, and sipped again. "Look around for anything you need, Irene, and help yourself. There's easy food and some drinks in the fridge."

"Okay. Anyone need anything? Tea sounds good to me." I'm actually hungry, but don't think I can hold food down right now. Later. Right now, I want to sit with my boy.

"There are some things Shay wants you to know, but talking wears him out."

I nod. "Anything. Whatever needs to be said." I'm scared at the possibilities of what might come next.

"Shay has choices of how to live his last days. He's chosen to wean off the pain meds to the best of his tolerance." Paul looks at Shane as he speaks, and I see the tears well up in his eyes.

Shane looks from Paul to me only moving his eyes, preserving his strength. "He wants to be as aware as possible. So he will be in a lot of pain, but you need to know that is what he chooses."

"Sweetheart, whatever you decide. This is yours, all yours. My plan is for you to know that I love you more than anything or one in this world. You can't go without knowing that...please."

"I'm going to take care of some things and leave you two alone. Okay?" I smile at Paul.

He knows how much I need to be alone with my son. The son who will leave me way too soon. My chest aches for what is lost and what is coming. I put a folded towel on his bony shoulder and lie my head there, as he drifts off to sleep. I don't move again until he wakes.

I think about the easy pregnancy with him and rubbing my huge stomach, feeling such love as I had never known. How adorable the chubby little guy was as he rolled over the first time, then managing to figure out crawling and then toddled and fell, achieving the amazing feat for such a little person...he walked. Only new parents understand those marvelous milestones. Maybe grandparents, but Shane didn't have any. I've never felt this close to him. But my heart aches like hell.

He wakes with a groan. "Mom?"

"I'm here."

He lets out a slight chuckle. "Thought maybe it was a dream," he whispers. "Do you remember when me and Russ caught that big-ass cat? Dad showed us how to clean it up and we ate it that night. It was as big as us. Ugliest damn thing I ever saw. I was afraid to swim in the lake until I forgot about it."

"I saw that ugly fish. Don't forget who had to fry it." We both smile at the memory.

"When was the last time I told you I love you?"

"Way too long." The tears roll and drip off my chin. "I'm sorry, I can't help it."

"No prob. I do it too. By the way, *I love you more than the Empire State Building.*"

"Oh my god. You remember that? I haven't heard you say that in years and I loved it when you'd tell me."

"We're having some people over tonight, Mom. And, there are some things I want to do before the end. I want you to be with me for all of it. You brought me into this crazy world, I feel blessed that you'll share this with me. I know it will be hard, but..."

"I'm here for whatever you need. I can take it, even if it might not look like it. I couldn't be anywhere else, right now, but here with you."

So I read Edgar Allen Poe to Shane, while Paul is swooshing around the kitchen area getting ready for tonight when their friends will come. He refuses my help, "You need to be with Shay." His name for my son no longer irritates me. I'm glad. I feel sort of peaceful here. I guess it's because Shane is. He is enjoying this. I read Poe to him as a child...weird little kid liked it, wasn't the least scared. I smile at the memory. So many memories, I hope we have time to recall many more.

"Lordy, Paul, this place is smelling good. I'm feeling hungry." Shane laughs because he has had no desire to eat in a long time. Paul comes over to tempt him with some raw shrimp. "Make sure you grill mine. Don't trust him, Mom. He's liable to sneak some of his raw stuff on your plate." Paul kissed his forehead. "For you, my love, anything."

Okay, I'm a little shocked. So what. Get over it, already. If Paul was Paula, I wouldn't be shocked, so that's my issue, and right now it doesn't count.

"Paul, if you'd get things ready, I can help Shane freshen up."

"Sure. But I'll have to help with dressing him. He loves being waited on, don't you?" Paul teased.

"See why I have to wear a beard? Gotta remind him who is the mucho macho around here."

~.~

Shane is laughing at his friends. Their goofiness is contagious. They help Paul move Shane into the recliner and then start with decorating, as if this happens every day. Balloons are hanging all around the rooms, held up by helium. Jan, Gary and Doc are sucking up helium and laughing like drunken ducks. I think I love each of these loyal friends who have come to make my son laugh and feel joy. He's in pain, but he is alive.

I watch them and listen as I strip the hospital-bed which will not be use, again. Shane will stay in the recliner. I throw on a bright green spread, one of Shane's favorite colors. I am so happy to be here, enjoying life with my son while we can.

The landlord comes in and hands his tiny puppy cockapoo to Shane. "Feels nice and fuzzy but it still smells like a damn dog," says Shane. The landlord, Dave, laughs and takes back his dog. The room is crowded. Friends, both male and female are kind to me, "So glad to finally meet you," and all that stuff. I've met some of them during past visits. But, I see their love for him. I know something new about my son. This is where he needed to be, where he could learn to be himself, surrounded by beautiful, loving friends. It feels strange to think this way but I am happy for him.

Paul leans over and whispers. Shane shakes his head and waves Paul away with a smile. I feel Paul's concern. The person we all love is in a lot of pain. Music is playing, mostly jazz. "I want to dance," he yells. Paul and two massive guys, whose names I want to remember, hold Shane up and sway to the sound of *Wonderful World*. A girl sat with me, arms around me, and we swayed together, too. For now, the world is a wonderful place.

~.~

"How was your night?" I ask him the next morning. I won't tell him that there was no sleep for his mother in the bedroom. I was up often checking. Sometimes Paul would be up with him, whispering to each other.

"I took something for pain around three this morning so I could get a little sleep. This is my last day, Mom." I can only nod and bite my lower lip. "Hey, my bros are going to be calling here in a little while. I'll kick their asses if they wait too late."

"I'll help you." I hold both his hands. I won't let go of him all day if I can help it. The phone rings and he smiles.

Your Cadillac is waiting, me lord." Paul makes a grand sweep as Doc and a few others come in with a fully equipped wheel chair. Today is his last day and he will spend it outside at his favorite places. Although I had not thought ahead about this, an ambulance is waiting for us in front of the apartment building. Paul is amazing. Thinks of everything.

Shane is hooked up to something...I don't ask. Doc, whether he is or not, is in the ambulance with myself, Paul, and of course, Shane. He is in great spirits this early afternoon. I hold his left hand while Paul holds the right.

How did it come to this? I try to stay in good spirits to match my son, but the pain is catching up to me. No pain pill can touch this hurt. I'm afraid I will fail him in these last hours...I've got to be strong, or pretend like hell.

He squeezes my hand. "Mom, I know." We cry together until the doors open and we are basking in the sun. The beach is heavenly. Blankets are close to the water so Shane can feel and smell the salty beauty of the ocean. His friends put up umbrellas and I see the sadness in their eyes. They stop now and then to hug each other. They planned well, as one or more of his friends rotate to sit with me and Shane, we're never alone.

"You know how much I love the lake, Mom? I love the beach even more. It's bigger than the imagination can comprehend without a map. This is the very spot where Paul will throw my ashes to the wind. I'll swim the ocean for eternity. I can't think of anything better than that."

"That's perfect, Shay." He looks into my eyes and smiles.

"You're alright, Mom. The best."

~.~

He sleeps on the way home, and even while his friends move him to the recliner. Doc is moving around preparing things that I don't want to see. I need some time for me. "God, I'm tired. Give me the strength to make it through this." The hot, wet cloth feels refreshing on my face. My hair is a mess, blown around by the wind all day at the beach. For Shane, the day was and is perfect. Maybe we all should be able to plan our last days and minutes. There is a peace in it.

Shane wakes and looks around for Paul and me. He nods to Doc, who waits for Shane's signal. Tubes run from a plastic bag to my son's arm. I feel like my throat is collapsing. Shane is weak and his eyes have no spark. Paul and I share the space at Shane's left. I kiss his cheek and forehead. Paul does the same and takes my hand to join our three hands. The room grows silent. My son leaves us to continue on. I'm alone.

Doc rests his hand softly on Shane's shoulder. "See 'ya on the other side, my friend."

Masques
By Brenda Drexler

The pure, open heart eager for love,

Sadly,

How can love be true,

Honest,

When it is only a minor player

In the grand production.

Whether it is that sanguine truth

That courses through the fragile veins

To the very core of the heart and soul,

To breathe in the gold, frankincense and myrrh

Of salvation to the hungry vessel.

Where is that omniscient lie-detector,

The guide, the guardian angel of knowledge

Of emotion, of life, the protector of

The heart that has been seduced and ravaged

By the past and present.

It was not in the readings of Dick and Jane and Spot,

Nor in the music of the time, which spoke of

Romance.

The truth is hidden behind the lie,

Masques of carnival,

Colorful and plumed, where every woman is a contessa,

For the night,

And every man a lord.

Masks disguising the face beneath, hidden by

Dark alleyways and the promises of the world outside.

A time of feast and pleasure, and little truth.

For truth does not unfold in the daring jumps

From the French balconies over Bourbon Street

Into the outstretched arms of revelers below, singing,

Trust me, trust me.

Alas, the truth unfolds in the cresting waves below,

In the cold wetness of the huge lake that swallows,

And grants asylum to whatever

And whoever dares to visit its cold depths.

And this is where the damaged soul, ripped and singed,

seeks solace,

When all the masks are removed

And the emptiness revealed.

Only a lake so deep and wide could

Offer such deep sanctuary to the damaged soul

that sought

The

embrace

of

serenity.

About the Author

Thanks for stopping by

Brenda Drexler's newest book of short stories is published. No joke. Go to **Amazon.com/author/brendadrexlerwriting** to find it.

Or, maybe you are reading it now, Life in Its Own Frame of Reference, 2016.

Brenda Drexler, is an author, teacher, Psychotherapist, wife, mother, grandmother, sister, yada, yada, yada...(thanks Elaine)...and has always had a passion for writing and reading and people and their relationships. She had to semi-retire to be able to dedicate the time and energy she wanted for writing. Good decision. She loves writing.

Brenda works her word-magic, humble as she is, in her home office in Southern Indiana, although she does admit to being a transplant from Louisville, KY.

Her first book of short stories, **Four Shorts for Your Bucket List,** can be found on Amazon as a Kindle book and paperback.

One of her short stories, **Marta**, can be found in **THE WORST BOOK IN THE UNIVERSE**, an Indian Creek Anthology, along with other authors from the Southern Indiana Writers Group. The target audience for this anthology is middle school age children, but any age would enjoy these great stories.

GRACIE AND MARGE: KICKING THE BUCKET TOGETHER is Brenda's first novel. Is it okay to say that she simply loves her main characters? They were born in one of her short stories, also found in her book **Four Shorts**. Some people have compared this novel to THELMA and LOUISE, but Brenda says that Gracie and Marge have a lot more sense than to drive off a cliff when there is so much life to be lived.

More books and short stories upcoming.

Brenda is available to visit and, perchance, read for local book clubs who have read one of her books. Contact Brenda: Brenda.writing@outlook.com. She would love to hear from you.

Made in the USA
Middletown, DE
27 July 2018